WHIRLWIND

RACHEL HATCH BOOK EIGHT

L.T. RYAN

with

BRIAN SHEA

LIQUID MIND MEDIA

THE RACHEL HATCH SERIES

Drift

Downburst

Fever Burn

Smoke Signal

Firewalk

Whitewater

Aftershock

Whirlwind

Tsunami

Fastrope

Sidewinder (Coming Soon)

RACHEL HATCH SHORT STORIES

Fractured

Proving Ground

The Gauntlet

Join the LT Ryan reader family & receive a free copy of the Rachel Hatch story, Fractured. Click the link below to get started:

https://ltryan.com/rachel-hatch-newsletter-signup-1

Love Hatch? Noble? Maddie? Cassie? Get your very own Jack Noble merchandise today! Click the link below to find coffee mugs, t-shirts, and even signed copies of your favorite L.T. Ryan thrillers! https://ltryan. ink/EvG_

ONE

Evelyn Mann took two steps inside the general store and stopped, allowing herself a moment to shake off the chill of the late spring morning. The phone had rung three times in less than ten minutes. The first call had been from the school principal informing her that her fifteen-year-old son, Trevor—a sophomore at Hawk's Landing High, and a permanent member of the principal's detention club—had had a behavioral outburst.

The principal hemmed and hawed his way through retelling what had happened. Trevor had flipped his desk when they confiscated his cell phone. His behavior during English class earned him a two-day suspension. Mann pleaded for leniency, but the principal held his ground, further explaining her son's Individualized Education Plan, his IEP. Her son had anger mitigation strategies to avoid outbursts, but when disruption was deemed "beyond mitigation," or, as Mann interpreted it, "beyond wanting to help at the moment," the plan of action was to send him home.

This would be the third time this year her son had been sent home. Mann had to be prepared for any disruptions in his schedule or otherwise. For the next two days, until the weekend hit, she would be on high alert to make sure that none of the inconsistencies of his daily routine would trigger another emotional breakdown. Great! She'd wanted to scream but opted for a frustrated sigh and a promise to pick him up within the next half hour.

Before she had stuffed her phone back into her purse, it rang again. The next incoming call was her ex-husband, a man who always seemed to time when Mann felt her lowest and find a way to make it worse.

Her high-school-sweetheart-turned-cheating-bastard left town over three years ago and in that time had barely made contact with his son, aside from a random phone call. Out of sight for over three years, only stopping by two Christmases ago and even then, he neglected to bring a gift.

Mann wasn't about taking handouts, but she'd reasoned guys like Chad were why deadbeat laws were established in the first place. She'd stayed home to raise their son with Asperger's. Before the diagnosis was made, he was a challenging baby and toddler, to say the least. Not that she had much of a career, but she was working her way to manager at the diner.

When they'd married, Chad had a decent job at the engineering company until they parted ways when he found a younger model with less baggage. He called at various times from different numbers, often switching carriers and numbers without telling her for several months. This, of course, made it impossible for Trevor to speak with his father even if he wanted to. Most of the time, he did not.

But here he was, calling as he always would after any type of issue with Trevor, as if her parenting wasn't enough. Maybe it wasn't, but damn it! He had left her high and dry and now he was two months late on child support.

Although she never used the money as a source of punishment, she wanted to. Hoping to sever any financial strings attached to the divorce, she'd applied for an assistant baker position. As of right now, she was late for the interview. She'd tried to call her potential employer, but the school interrupted, so here she was. Taking a moment to compose herself and shake off the cold, she now had to stare at the ringing phone from her ex-husband. He would call her again and again until she answered. He always did.

She entered the grocery store and noticed the bakery section was on the far right. Mann saw the head baker was busy with an older gentleman at the counter. While Mann made her way over, she decided to answer the call and put a quick end to whatever he was calling for.

"Chad," she said, her tone quiet but harsh. "I don't want to hear it. I'm not in the mood and I'm late for a job interview."

"Whoa, babe. Why do you always gotta give me such a hard time? How come I can't just call and check in?"

"Because you never call and check in. We have to track you down. I'm just shocked that this is the same number you called me from last time."

"Listen, I know I've been spotty with the paychecks, but I was just calling to tell you I'm getting it to you soon."

"Do you know how many times I've heard that? 'Don't worry about it. It's just around the corner,' you'll take care of everything, you'll make things right? Blah, blah, blah. I'm done with it, Chad. I don't need you or your money anymore. I don't need you to remember Trevor's birthday, which you've forgotten the last two years. We don't need you. There was a time when we did. There was a time when you were my world, and I thought everything was right, and now that I see you for who you are, I couldn't be happier that you're gone.

"And trust me, Trevor's going through a tough time. I know you called to rub it in and you're twisting it now like you always do. But let me tell you this, Trevor's going to be fine, too. We need to rid ourselves of the baggage holding us back, and that's you. After this call, the next thing you'll hear is from my attorney and I will get full custody of our son until he turns eighteen. But you will no longer be a part of our lives. Do you understand me?"

"Sure, but you talk like this a lot, too. Always threatening me. Why do you think I have to switch phones so much? Why do I have to change addresses?"

"Because you can't hold a job, Chad. Not since you left." Silence for a moment.

Mann could tell her words hit the mark. He was probably in between jobs now, and he was probably calling just before this cell carrier dropped him, just like a few months back. It was always the same story, shrouded in the same lie. The difference in the man she'd fallen for at sixteen, now thirty-nine, was day and night.

"Goodbye Chad. You're free of us now." Mann clicked "end" on the phone and slid it back into her purse as she moved towards the bakery. She recognized the old man at the counter chatting the baker's ear off. It was her son's psychologist, Glenn Miller. He'd been a godsend for Trevor. They'd only started a few months back, but she'd seen a dramatic improvement in her son's ability to control his outbursts. Miller recently offered to try Trevor on hypnotherapy, something the psychologist claimed to have worked in the past with tremendous results. The irony was not lost on Mann that she was now standing behind him after receiving the call from the school. Something that would no doubt be addressed in Trevor's next session.

Mann checked her watch. It was just a few minutes past nine. She hoped her interview with the baker moved along quicker than the conversation he was having with Miller. Making eye contact with the baker, she smiled. He gave a subtle nod toward Miller, which Mann took to mean: "Whenever Mr. Miller is done, we'll proceed with the interview."

Mann felt her phone vibrating once again. Unzipping her purse, she looked down. It was Chad again. Since hanging up on him she had missed three calls. Now she ignored it once more and zipped her purse back up.

She wasn't kidding this time. She was done with him, done with the games. She wouldn't call him back again and she'd honor her word as she'd meant to time and time again. Mann was deep in thought when someone bumped her from behind, almost knocking her purse off her shoulder.

Mann turned to see the vacant stare of a messy haired kid only a few years older than her son. Rail thin, he wore a short-sleeved white button-up and matching colored pants. Even his lace-less sneakers were white. The boy's attire reminded Mann of the milkmen of old.

The boy in white stopped a foot behind Miller. She listened close and could hear him speaking, but Mann couldn't make it out over the sound of Miller's voice. He mumbled the same word over and over.

Staring at the odd young man, she noticed his right hand. At first, she thought it was an oversized cell phone like the ones you'd see in the 80s, and then she realized the large black item in his hand was a pistol.

The boy continued muttering as he raised the weapon and pointed it at the center of Miller's back.

Mann watched in horror as the first shot rang out. She stood frozen as Miller fell face first onto the floor. The boy fired the gun five more times. He stood rigid, the gun still pointing at the lifeless body of her son's psychologist. His finger continued to pull the trigger of the empty revolver.

Click…click…click.

Mann fled out of the store, into the parking lot where the other employees and patrons had gathered. Sirens could be heard in the distance.

She could see through the front window that the boy in white had not moved. In her head she could still hear the rhythmic strike of the revolver's hammer into the empty cylinder.

Click…click…click.

TWO

HATCH STOOD A FEW FEET FROM THE LONG, PARALLEL STEEL BARS SET AT chest height. The bars extended for about fifteen feet and marked the start point to the Basic Underwater Demolition SEAL training obstacle course.

Working her arms in small circles to warm up her shoulders, she bent and flexed her knees as Banyan set out the rules for the course.

"Timer starts as soon as you touch the bars. You get two tries on every obstacle. Fail the second time and it's a no-go. Every time you go over the Hooyah logs, you need to interlace your fingers behind your head. When you get to the forty-foot tower, it's your choice how to descend. First phase you have to go feet first, but after that, you can ranger crawl it."

Hatch scanned the expanse of the sandy beach. Unlike Nasty Nick, tucked deep into the North Carolina woods, its obstacles obscured by high trees, she could see all the obstacles before her. It was intimidating when trying to look at everything, so Hatch focused on the first task.

"Once the timer starts, you have twelve minutes to complete all eleven obstacles and get back here."

Hatch nodded. What started over beers would end here on the

sand. She checked the laces on her boots and tucked her BDU pants inside. She wore a long-sleeved shirt and they gave her the option of wearing a shock resistant helmet, but she opted not to.

Hatch stood ready, tuning out the back-and-forth trash talking between Banyan and Cruise. A light mist descended as Hatch gripped the parallel bars. She knew the timer on Banyan's watch had started, and so had the one running in her own head.

She hoisted herself onto the bars. Bicycling her legs, she shimmied across the fifteen feet to the other side quickly. Approaching the low wall, she used the stump in front of it to vault over to the high wall. The high wall's wood surface was already coated in the mist and the wood was now slick to the touch, too high for Hatch to jump over the seven-foot-two wall, but it had a thick rope hanging at its center.

Hatch gave a two-step lunge, grabbing the rope midway and pulling herself up and over the wall. The light rain dampened the sand and kept it from getting in her face and eyes as she dropped to her belly and began low crawling under the barbed wire. Pulling herself through the sandy pit, she faced off with a fifty-foot cargo net.

Though she had faced her fear of heights at her father's hand, time and time again during her service in the military, and most recently on an Alaskan mountaintop, Hatch still had to face the same fear every time. Each time, she had to find her workaround for coping.

She'd had plenty of experience with the cargo net. Eyes straight ahead, look at the rope right in front of you. And she did, ascending one of the cargo lines, using the vertical knots in front of her as her handholds, taking two or three rungs at a time with her feet. She ascended the fifty feet and then hoisted herself over the other side, trying to keep her head upright, looking at the horizon. She made quick work to the bottom.

A zigzag of uneven bars rolled, but Hatch moved fast and maintained her balance. She felt she was making good time as she did a rope exchange, climbing one twelve-foot rope and then reaching across to descend on another. Her gut was tested on an obstacle known as the Ugly Name.

She had to jump from one horizontal timber to another. The

second timber was a few feet higher and several feet further. She saw the only way to effectively go over the higher log was to jump hard and take the impact at the waist, which Hatch did. The thick log's curved side slammed hard into her stomach, causing her to curse as she rolled her body forward and over the painful obstacle.

She navigated the Weaver with relative ease, the staple obstacle of many courses she'd run before. She then encountered another set of the Hooyah logs. The stack of logs rising five timbers high were staggered throughout. She used it to catch her breath before encountering the next obstacle.

The Burma Bridge had a twenty-foot rope hanging down on one end. Hatch ascended it and came to a three-rope bridge where the knots between the connections widened as the bridge extended across the sand. Hatch used her long legs to her advantage as she crossed the bridge.

On the other side, she looked at the obstacle awaiting her, the Forty-Foot Tower, a four-story wooden structure open on all sides. At the very top, a long thick rope extended down to the sand at a forty-five-degree angle. Hatch jogged up on the obstacle and took a moment to catch her breath. Her arms and legs burned. A metallic taste filled her mouth and she spit it into the wet sand.

Hatch reached up. The lip of the first tier was just out of reach. Hatch would have to jump and then swing her leg on the outside. With the soft sand slightly packed from the rain, she bent her legs and sprung up. Gripping hard with her left hand and digging her fingernails into the wood, she kicked her left leg up hard and over, using the momentum of her jump. She clawed her way onto the first level of the tower.

Now, inside the tower structure, she had to reach out. Again, she could only touch the bottom, not the top lip. She positioned herself at the edge, keeping her left hand ready. And just like on the ground, she bent her knees and shot up, grabbing at the rung.

She kicked her leg hard. The side of her boot hit the outside wood, knocking her off balance. Her fingers slipped. She let go and tried to catch herself on the first level, but fell back-flat onto the packed sand below. The impact knocked the wind out of Hatch.

She exhaled. Rolling to her side, she punched the sand, angry at herself. She took two short breaths in, clearing her mind, and reset at the base of the tower. Just like she had done before, she navigated to the first level. This time, Hatch made sure not to underestimate the effort needed to get beyond.

Everything grew quiet. Her only focus was on the floor just above her. Hatch bent deep and then shot her arm upwards, kicking hard and wide. The momentum carried her up and over. Her left arm fatigued from the effort. She switched to her right side. Hatch repeated the process, lunging to the third floor. She felt the tingle in her scarred right arm as she worked her way to her knees.

The fourth and final tier that would take her to the top of the tower required her to go through an open shoot door at the top. To do so, Hatch had to jump and catch the upper lip of the top tier with both elbows, then swing her bent knee through. Catching herself with her heels, she rolled to the right.

On her knees, at the top of the forty-foot tower, the wind from the Pacific Ocean just beyond the high sand berms pushed a breeze across. Hatch worked herself over on her hands and knees to the rope extending down. She lay belly flat on the wet wood surface and pulled herself out.

As her right knee came off the top landing of the tower, she draped her ankle across the wire rope, stabilizing herself as she descended. Her left leg hung loose and acted as a counterbalance to the shifts of her body weight. Hatch made quick work getting to the bottom. The remaining obstacles posed little challenge in the way of difficulty.

Her biggest hurdle behind her, Hatch now focused on time as she crossed a rope swing, moved across a set of monkey bars, navigated a short obstacle hurdle, and then used her fingertips and the edges of her boot to scale a spider wall before dropping into a dead sprint across the sand to the finish line where Banyan and Cruise waited.

As Hatch ran to the two, Banyan called time. Hatch dropped her hands to her knees and took two big inhales. "How'd I do?" Hatch gasped between ragged breaths.

"8:34," Banyan said, looking at his watch.

Cruise held out his hand. "Pay up. A bet's a bet."

Words had obviously been exchanged during Hatch's navigation of the obstacle course. This was evident by the roll of Banyan's eyes as he fished out his wallet.

"Banyan's just mad because you almost beat his best time."

Banyan's face reddened.

"Not everyone runs it in six minutes." Cruise tapped the cane against his braced right leg, the damage done during their last op in Alaska. "I think those days are long gone. I'm not an Honor Man like you."

"Those days are never gone."

"But come to think of it, I'll take you on a double or nothing."

Banyan ran his thumb across the money in his billfold and cocked a curious eye at Cruise.

"I bet Hatch here can best your time. Shoot, all she has to do is drop two seconds. If she hadn't fallen off that second tier of the tower, she would've had you."

"Whoa!" Hatch threw up her hands, taking a big inhale of the cool morning air. "Who said I'd ever run that thing again? Remember, this all started because you guys wanted to know which obstacle course was tougher."

"And the verdict?" Banyan asked.

"Nasty Nick is everything as nasty as they say. But if I'm being honest, this course provides some X factors I've never seen anywhere else. The sand makes it a totally different challenge. And that tower almost got me."

"About that," Banyan said. "You tried to go up by swinging your leg to the side. A lot of guys do it, but there's an easier way. Not all of us are tall drinks of water like your friend Cruise here. Guys like me, in the Smurf crew, we had to adapt and overcome."

Banyan was four inches shorter than Hatch, so about five-foot-six. "The way to do it with minimal effort and best success is to start deeper, underneath each tier, and jump and grab with both hands on the lip, swinging your legs underneath you, using the momentum of both legs to pull you up and over, like an intense kip-up."

"I'll keep it in mind. But as of right now, don't bet on me running this again."

Cruise opened his mouth to speak when the cell phone in his hand vibrated. He'd been holding it for Hatch and handed it to her. She flicked it open.

"It's Tracy."

The message from Jordan Tracy, Talon Executive Services Commander, read, "Brief at ten?"

Hatch messaged back, "RGR."

She looked up at Cruise. "Briefing at ten."

"Oh, the Bat signal has sounded. Don't want to keep you from your secret lair," Banyan cut in.

"Banyan's not a big fan of private contract work. He'd rather help midlife crisis males and overweight homebodies try to get their SEAL shape on." Cruise teased.

"Hey." Banyan raised his hand in defense. "I'm doing my part to make people at the beaches look better. It's a public service, really. The world can thank me later."

Cruise looked at his watch and then checked his phone.

"No message?" Hatch asked.

He shook his head no. "Strange."

Hatch got another message. It was the name of a café. "Stranger, the briefing is not at the office."

Banyan pulled out his money to pay his bet. Cruise put his hand out, refusing it. "I'd still like to keep the double or nothing on the table."

"Keep it on the table all you want," Hatch said. "You're not getting me back on that tower."

THREE

THE PEN STOPPED WHERE IT ALWAYS DID. THE PART WHERE HE STARTED to write the three words he'd never had the heart to say but always wished he had. For spending such little time with someone, he had never thought about anyone more in his life. As he set the pen down, this would be another letter to Rachel Hatch that he never finished.

He sipped his coffee. Hatch's mother, Jasmine, had made him a thermos-full when he had stopped by earlier that morning to check on the kids and say, "Hi." Something he did whenever he was close, and sometimes when he wasn't. In the absences between Hatch's comings and goings, he had taken on the role of surrogate father or uncle for the kids, and Jasmine Hatch doted on him like a son.

Savage set the letter aside on his desk. He traded his pen for the thermos and took a long pull of Jasmine's brew.

His cell phone rang as his radio came to life. The radio always took priority. When he had taken over as Sheriff of Hawk's Landing, he said that both his cell and radio would be accessible twenty-four hours a day.

"Sheriff Savage? Sheriff Savage, are you there?" He had tried to get everybody in his small department onto a code system similar to the one Denver PD used, but it hadn't taken.

"Go ahead Barbara. What do you got?" Savage said, draining the last of his coffee, figuring this call would take him late into the night.

"It's at Westin's Grocery. Some crazy with a gun went in and shot Glenn Miller. I mean, somebody shot to death a 72-year-old man standing in a grocery store! This is Hawk's Landing, not Los Angeles!" Her voice was on edge.

"Barbara, I need you to tell me, where is the shooter now? What's the situation on scene at this moment?"

"Chaos. But the caller I spoke with said he fired the gun until empty, but he didn't take aim at anyone else. And he didn't run."

"He's still on scene?"

"Caller said he's standing there with the gun in his hand. He hasn't moved."

"Is anybody else hurt or wounded?"

"No. An older woman was knocked down as shoppers fled."

Savage was already in his SUV and speeding toward town center where the Westin's was located. "Besides Miller and the shooter, is there anybody else still inside?"

"No. I've got the caller on the line and will keep you posted."

Savage keyed the mic. "Sinclair, did you copy?"

"Already on my way." Sirens blared in the background.

"As long as the shooter remains inside and there are no other reports of gunfire, you hold on the outside and wait for me before entering."

"Yessir."

"The second that changes and the shooting becomes active again, you're going in. With or without me. Understood?"

"Yessir." This time, her voice was less resolute.

"Hold the perimeter. And whatever you do, do not let him leave." Tires squealed as he took a hard right. "I'm on my way."

Savage tore down the winding mountain roads and headed into the downtown area of Hawk's Landing. As he turned onto Main Street, he could see the siren lights flickering. He navigated his way around some pedestrian bystanders looking on from a distance and found a spot next to Sinclair's squad car. She was standing outside with her gun in front of her, pointing to the storefront.

There was no sign of the man with the gun, but they maintained a loosely held perimeter out of the sheer fear and panic of the moment. Savage walked toward it all. He never ran, always taking his steps carefully to process the scene, making sure the shooter hadn't slipped out and pretended to be a bystander. He made sure there was no odd man out. Seeing none, he proceeded to Sinclair's position.

"Nothing?"

"Nothing since the call came in."

"We need to move in now. We have to open the line of communication and render lifesaving aid to the downed man."

"But the shooter killed him. "

"I don't care if they shot him with a bazooka. Until I confirm life or death, I'm assuming he's alive, and we're going to try to bring him out as such."

"Understood, sir."

"Stack up. We're moving."

Savage and Sinclair pressed forward, moving with their weapons tight against their chests, sighted in the direction of the known threat. Sirens bounced off the neighboring buildings as Littleton's squad car screeched to a halt on the other side of the road. The lanky deputy sprinted awkwardly toward them and joined their gaggle just as they entered the store.

An eerie silence cast out the chaos of the terrified citizenry on the outside of the doors. Soft elevator music played over a PA system. They moved slowly, using the aisles for cover. Savage at the lead, he cleared each one before stepping to the next, moving ever closer to the bakery area.

He moved soft shoe, rolling his heel along the outside to his toes, a trick he'd learned from one of his partners who'd done a stint in the military. He could hear Littleton and Sinclair trying, but failing, to move noiselessly behind him, into the last barrier where aisle one and two divided.

He leaned against the fresh garden veggies open refrigeration unit and could feel the cool blast of mist showering the produce. Through the baker's door across the way, Savage glimpsed the shooter in the reflection of the glass. He stood still in a white short-sleeve button-up and white denim pants. He was looking forward and down, the opposite direction from Savage and his team.

Savage held his non-gun hand behind his head and began a countdown with his fingers: *three, two, one.*

He stepped wide, bringing the weapon up to target and began barking orders in a loud, controlled tone.

"You in the white shirt, drop the weapon. This is Dalton Savage, Hawk's Landing Sheriff. I have three guns trained on you. We do not want to hurt you!"

Nothing. Silence. Except for the repetitive click of the trigger.

The shooter continued looking down at the floor, soaked slick with Glenn Miller's blood. There was no doubt Miller was dead from the amount of blood spreading out. Rendering aid was a moot point. Surviving the deadly encounter now took precedent.

"Drop the gun. Now!" Simple commands, simple words.

Sinclair shifted her position and stumbled. She knocked into a rack of potato chips, sending the rack and its contents to the floor. The loud bang of the metal hitting against the hard floor, startled the shooter. Like a starter pistol, the boy in white seemed to come out of a trance, looking around as if he'd just woken from a nightmare.

His stunned gaze shifted from Sinclair as she recovered to lock eyes with Savage.

Savage saw a fleeting look of horror on the young face. The weapon fell from his hand and clattered loudly to the floor beside him.

In the minutes that followed, while Savage's team took the shooter into custody, the boy didn't utter a single word. Savage looked through the rear window of Sinclair's cruiser, noticing the white clothing dotted with the spatter of Miller's blood.

The young shooter sat with his back rigid and stared ahead at the wired cage separating him from the vehicle's front compartment. Only his trigger finger moved, rhythmically tapping his knee.

Tap...tap...tap.

FOUR

HATCH ARRIVED AT THE CAFÉ A FEW MINUTES BEFORE TEN. IT WAS SET among the bars and restaurants of San Diego's Gaslamp district. Several outdoor dining areas had their lamps lit. Even in the six weeks that had passed since her time in Breakneck, Hatch still felt the chill of Alaska in the cool California breeze.

As she entered the quaint café, she saw Jordan Tracy already there, sitting in the far-right corner of the restaurant with his back against the wall. Sipping his coffee, he waved to Hatch as she crossed the floor.

"Sorry to pull you away from your morning," Tracy said.

"You didn't interrupt anything. I just finished a workout on the beach," Hatch replied.

"That sand plays hell on your legs."

"Tell me about it." Hatch rubbed her thighs, still feeling the tingle of the O-course.

"Cruise put you up to it?"

"You could say that."

"He took me on some of his beach runs, though I'm more of a pavement or backwoods runner myself. How's he doing, by the way?" Tracy asked.

"Good as possible. His latest physical therapist hasn't quit yet, so that's a good sign."

"Cruise will push the pedal until he's out of gas."

"That's what makes him who he is."

"You're not far off his mark."

Hatch shrugged off the compliment.

"How'd he take not getting the message?" Tracy asked.

"Good, I guess. Confused as I am." Hatch said.

"I'll clear it up with him later, but this one is off the books."

Hatch gave a slow nod.

"My niece went missing last night." Tracy divulged.

"Where?"

"She lives with her mom in a small town outside of Nashville. Jericho Falls, barely a blip on the map."

Hatch thought of her tiny town of Hawk's Landing and the big trouble that had found its way there. "Are the police involved?"

"Yeah, they're looking into it."

"So what do you want me to do?"

"I want you to be eyes on the ground for me. Make sure the investigation is in lockstep, that everything within their power is being done."

"And how do you suppose I go about that?"

Tracy slid across a thick envelope. Hatch reached inside and fished out a new driver's license and employment badge.

"Figured I'd use your name easier. Less worry about slip-up. Unless you prefer to use the alias you chose while in New Mexico? Daphne Nighthawk, was it?"

"How'd you know about that?"

"Talon had a pretty extensive file on you." He offered an apologetic smile. "The choice is yours. I can have my guy whip up new creds if you want."

"Using my name won't have repercussions?"

"None that I see. Everything else has been adjusted. The driver's license is clean, age-appropriate, and approximate. I put you living in Nashville. It's a big enough city for someone to be anonymous."

Hatch picked up the badge. A plastic, sealed laminate coating covered it and it had a metal clip to attach to her pocket or sleeve. It read, "Investigative Reporter, R. Hatch. The Blaze, Tennessee's independent voice for the people."

"I thought you said this op was off the books. Yet, you whipped up a backstory, some credentials, and an ID pretty fast."

"A lot of people owe me, so I collected on a favor or two. But as far as Talon's support, there won't be an overwatch. I'd go, but we're having Taylor's service this week and I'm attending to his wife and children."

Brad Taylor—the former special operator and Talon Executive Service triggerman—was taken out by a force of nature on the same Alaskan mountaintop that had nearly claimed Hatch's life. She understood the heavy burden Tracy felt as commander, and the debt he shouldered in honoring his responsibility to Taylor's family.

"This wouldn't even register on Talon's threat matrix, and if we started deploying our assets willy-nilly, even for family, we'd overstep our reach and undermine our sole purpose. But that's not to say you're not going in unprotected. That backstory is clean. If they investigate you, The Blaze is an online news agency. There's a full website, several articles written in your name, and the number goes straight to me. As far as funding goes, I will take care of everything. I've already arranged the airfare and rental car."

Hatch blinked and shook her head in astonishment. "Why me?"

"Not considering your performance in salvaging what was otherwise a failed operation, your military police background would serve this situation best. My guys are hit-them-and-forget-them operators. You come with a different set of skills, and from what Cruise tells me, you're a hell of an interrogator."

"Thanks. So what should I know about your niece?"

"Her name is Kyla. She's twelve years old. Her mother is Dorothy Green. Kyla took her mother's maiden name. My brother Benjamin was in jail when she was born. In and out of prison for several years after. Hasn't had contact with Kyla in six years. Said he was trying to get a court order invoked for visitation rights."

"I hate to point this out," Hatch interrupted, "but in cases involving a domestic issue, when a child goes missing, the first place we have to look is the family. And if you're telling me, there is a custodial argument, I'd be looking at your brother first."

"My brother is the one who called me."

The waitress came by and refreshed Tracy's cup. Hatch flipped her mug for her own fill. The waitress asked if they wanted to order from the menu. Tracy said they needed a moment. The waitress then bounced her way around to her other tables.

Tracy let out a sigh and rubbed the gray of his temples. The seasoned operator reminded her of Dalton Savage, Hawk's Landing's sheriff and someone for whom Hatch cared deeply. She hadn't figured out where things stood with her and Cruise and it left her conflicted, furthering her state of limbo.

When it came to entering a room and handling an adversary, Hatch was smooth, cool as ice. When it came to handling the relationships in her personal life, Hatch was all thumbs. She felt the fumble and could do nothing to stop it.

She'd called Savage only once since Alaska, letting him know everything was okay, that she was safe, and that there were no more threats. He had asked her when she was coming home, and her answer had held true. She didn't know.

The thought thrummed in the back of her mind, a constant hum behind every step forward she took with Cruise. Quieting it, she focused on the man in front of her.

"I didn't even know I had a niece until last night."

Tracy stirred a spoonful of sugar into his cup, foregoing cream. He took a sip and continued. "All families aren't postcard perfect. My brother Ben, he's ten years younger than me, so our relationship was always a little strained. I felt more an uncle than a brother at times. When he got into the drugs and started stealing from our family, I tried to intervene. The last time I talked to him ended in blows. We hadn't spoken in fifteen years. So I'm playing catch-up myself. All I know is that my brother said he's clean, and that at some point during the chaos of their relationship, during one of his stints at either rehab or prison, his on-again-off-again girlfriend and mother to his daughter joined a religious group known as The Eternal Light."

"What kind of religious group?" Hatch asked.

"I pawed through the internet to see what I could find out. Not much there at all, really. Just a small piece in an out-of-print newspaper from fifteen years back when the group moved into town. The little that was written suggested the group's belief structure, while founded in Christianity, crosses with a lot of elemental stuff in the preachings of their leader.

"Do we know anything about him?"

"Only that he goes by The Shepherd. Other than that, I couldn't locate a name or picture to ID him."

"When did Kyla go missing?"

"All Ben knows is that he tried to serve the custodial papers. He said he couldn't get through to see his ex, Dorothy Green, but that he had seen Kyla. When he tried to get her attention by calling to her, he was escorted from the property. He went back the next day with a police escort, only to find that she was missing."

"Then the clock is ticking. When do I leave?"

"Your flight is in three hours. I just sent you everything I have in a secure email. Included is a picture of Kyla that Ben got from the sheriff. This is Kyla." Tracy tapped his phone and turned it to Hatch.

She looked at the image. A girl in pigtails, a white dress, and light brown hair with sun-bleached ends. She was smiling and one tooth was missing. Hatch looked at the little girl and immediately thought of Daphne, her own niece.

She returned the phone to Tracy and slid the ID back into the envelope. She looked at her reporter identification and thought of the brave reporter from Juarez. Hatch slid it inside and drained the rest of her coffee.

"I better get going."

"Remember Hatch, this is just an intel op. If you get something helpful, I want you just to forward it to the investigating agency. I want to stay off the radar in this one but help in any way that I can. No shitstorms."

"I understand, and I'll do what I can to find your niece."

A breeze blew in from the east, carrying the briny saltiness of the nearby ocean on it as Hatch walked out of the diner. With her old name and new identity tucked under her arm, she was off to find the niece Jordan Tracy never knew he had.

FIVE

SAVAGE SAT AT HIS DESK AND WATCHED THE MONITOR RELAYING surveillance footage from inside the interrogation room where the shooter sat, still wearing his white clothes. His hands and ankles were shackled to a bolt in the floor.

Since arriving at the Hawk's Landing Sheriff's Office, the shooter had said nothing. Not a word while they took his fingerprints using the AFIS machine, the Automated Fingerprint Identification System used worldwide.

Long gone were the days since Savage had to ink roll people's hands and wait several weeks or months for an identity. Now those answers came in a matter of minutes, but it was lagging a bit, and so Savage had their shooter placed in the interrogation room while they waited.

The room was comprised two chairs set on opposite sides of a square table. The shooter sat half facing the camera system in the upper right corner and away from the door. He didn't move. He didn't look towards the camera, but stared straight ahead at the wall in front of him, his body rigid.

He had both hands stretched out, evenly spacing the links between them. His right index finger tapped against the metal table. At first,

Savage thought the tapping was an autonomic response, the brain recapturing that moment when he pulled the trigger six times into the torso of seventy-two-year-old Glenn Miller. Savage knew how many times he had replayed his own shootings, including the one that forced him to find refuge here in the mountains of La Plata County.

The brain, under traumatic stress, tried to replay, recalculate, and understand those scenarios. Some were stuck in a perpetual loop that disabled a person entirely. Savage had experienced his fair share of post-traumatic stress disorder. At first, he thought this was the reaction he was seeing, the tapping of the trigger finger, the remembrance of the six shots, the replay of why and how and where. But then, as he stared at the porcelain man, Savage noticed the bottom right screen where the time ticked by on the recorder. The boy's finger taps were in sync with the second hand of Savage's wristwatch.

The killer waited, counting the seconds. The door to Savage's office swung open. The loose hinge made it creak loudly and startled Savage. Sinclair stood there with several sheets of paper in her hand, holding them up high.

"You won't believe this. I swore I recognized him when we put the cuffs on him, but it just didn't make sense. I couldn't remember where I knew him. His name didn't come to me."

"Let's hope this guessing game isn't going to take much longer," Savage said, eagerly staring at the white sheets in her hand.

"That's Billy Graver," Sinclair said, as if the name was supposed to mean something to Savage.

He shrugged. "Who's Billy Graver?"

"You've never heard the story of the Gravers? You've never heard... I think Lifetime did one of those movies of the week on it."

Savage shook his head. "I was a city cop. I didn't watch Lifetime movies."

"I was older than Billy. This goes back ten years, but I believe he was twelve at the time. Hawk's Landing being so small, I knew him in passing. I remember him as being a bit odd. Sometimes he would talk to himself, always mumbling whatever word occupied his mind, repeating it over and over again. The papers said he was a genius.

Awareness about the Autism spectrum hadn't made its way out here to Hawk's Landing. We hadn't seen much of it, so we just thought he was, you know, crazy. Maybe he was abused and all, but his family had money. And he had a sister, a year younger."

"What happened to him?"

"Them." Sinclair's face grew darker. "They'd apparently gone for a walk. They took the same path every day, rain or shine. All part of Billy's routine, and his sister often accompanied him. Just before a really bad blizzard hit, they went out and didn't return.

"I remember the searches, joining them twice. The snow made it tough. On day five, the sheriff at the time shifted the efforts from rescue to recovery."

"How long until Billy and his sister were found?"

"Billy was found about a week later. A park ranger located him in a cave. Starved and near dead. Billy was covered in his sister's blood."

"What happened to her?" Savage asked.

"Amanda Graver's body was never found."

"Did Billy ever speak about it?"

"Not a word."

"Was he ever implicated?"

"No evidence besides his sister's blood. Without an ability to communicate, Billy was sent to a full-time care facility outside of Denver."

Savage looked at the monitor and the porcelain man tapping rhythmically. "Well, let's see if he'll talk today."

The Sheriff entered the interview room and approached the table where the twenty-two-year-old who looked more like a boy than a man sat. He was seemingly oblivious to the chaos of the morning's events and that of his current situation. Savage set the bag of chips and can of Sprite within arm's reach of Graver, who remained seated with the same rigid posture he had held since first entering the room. His eyes remained transfixed on the wall ahead of him, and his right index finger maintained its rhythmic tapping.

"I'm going to call you Billy because that's what Becky back there said she knew you by when you used to live here. If you'd prefer me to call you something else, please let me know. My name is Dalton Savage. I'm the sheriff here in Hawk's Landing, and I know you've been through a traumatic event. I'd like to talk to you about it, but I have to advise you of your rights, and make sure you understand those rights before we have a conversation."

The tapping continued. Graver's face remained placid, with no reaction. Savage continued. "All right, Billy. Well, I'm going to look for some sign of acknowledgment that you'd like to talk to me when I'm finished."

Graver met Savage's words with complete and utter silence.

"William Graver, you are under arrest and in custody for the shooting death of Glenn Miller. I would like to talk to you about the circumstances of that shooting. This is being recorded by the audio and video surveillance up there in the corner. You have the right to remain silent. Anything you say or do can be used against you in a court of law. You have the right to an attorney, and if you cannot afford an attorney, one will be provided to you by the state. And you have the right to not answer any of the questions I ask you. What I do have to know, right now is, do you understand your rights as I've advised them?"

The tapping continued. Billy's eyes never shifted right or left.

"Billy Graver, do you agree to speak with me?" Tap, tap, tap. "How can I help you? How can I find out if anything that happened in the store had to do with your sister Amanda's disappearance, if you don't talk to me?"

The tapping stopped. Graver's eyes shifted off the wall and met Savage's, as if waking up from a dream. Looking frantically around, his mouth opened to speak when the door buzzed and a short man wearing an expensive suit that bulged at the midriff barged in with Becky Sinclair hot on his tail.

"Mr. Graver is my client. His parents saw their son on the news. I'm the Graver family's legal counsel and will be representing William. At this point in time, my client will not be speaking to you. I will arrange to make myself available to you at a future time. Bail has already been posted with the court." The attorney handed the bond receipt to Savage. "I will be taking Mr. Graver with me now."

The attorney then clicked twice with what appeared to be a dog clicker. The frantic eyes of Billy Graver settled again, and the rhythmic tapping resumed. Two more clicks and Billy stood beside the short man, towering over him by at least six inches. Billy was pencil thin and the attorney portly, like an Abbott and Costello pairing without the humor. Savage looked on as Billy left the Hawk's Landing Sheriff's Office interrogation room, and the tapping of Billy's right index finger resumed alongside his pant leg, keeping time with the seconds.

Savage went to his office and sat for a moment, then he picked up the phone to call one of the witnesses from the Miller shooting.

"Screw you! I told you not to call me!"

"Miss Mann? It's Sheriff Savage. If I've called at a bad time, then—"

"Oh, sorry. I thought this was my ex-husband. He's always changing his number. Can't get himself together."

"Is it a problem I can help with?"

"Nothing criminal. Unless you count being a deadbeat." She sighed and caught her breath. "What can I help you with, Sheriff?"

"I know you've had a rough day, but I wanted to follow up. Even though you've been interviewed already, I was hoping to make sure we didn't miss anything. The brain can take time to pick up bits and pieces. Details that were overwhelmed by the freshness of events."

"Anything to help."

"Why don't you start by walking me through everything?"

"I was late for an interview. But it was okay, because when I arrived, the baker was distracted by a conversation with Glenn Miller. I was a bit distracted myself. My ex had called. Then the shooter bumped into me."

"And then what happened?" Savage could hear Mann's breathing change and wanted to keep her moving forward.

"He pulled a gun and started shooting."

"Did he say anything before he started?"

"No—Wait. Yes." There was a burst of energy from Mann. "He was mumbling something."

"Do you remember what he said?"

"I think he was saying, *protect him*. But I can't be sure. It was tough to hear him over Miller's conversation."

"Did it sound like he was saying it to Miller?"

"No, I don't think so. His voice was quiet, almost a whisper. He kept saying the words like a record on repeat."

Savage thought of the metronomic fashion in which Billy had tapped his pant leg when leaving and tapped the table to the rhythm of the second hand of a clock. Even his voice and the repetitious words were in synchronistic harmony with some internal clock.

"Did that help?" There was a desperateness to Mann's question.

"Yes." Savage then advised Mann that Deputy Sinclair would be by to get a written statement.

Savage ended the call and looked at the crime scene photos scattered across his desk. The 8x10 glossies bore the evidence of the violence that occurred in the grocery that morning. Six holes in the center of Miller's unsuspecting back put there by Billy Graver, the boy in white.

Protect him. Savage wasn't sure what it meant, but he wouldn't rest until he did. What was the connection between the disappearance of Amanda Graver and the death of Glenn Miller? For Savage, it was an itch he couldn't quite scratch.

SIX

H_ATCH MADE GOOD TIME AFTER HER MEETING WITH T_RACY IN downtown San Diego to Cruise's apartment in Coronado, over-looking the bay. He hung from a pull up bar set up on the back deck where he liked to get his workouts in while absorbing the California sunshine.

"Your physical therapist would kill you if he saw you on that bar."

Cruise paused his pullup at the top. His chest pressed against the bar as he turned his head to greet Hatch. "I won't tell if you don't. Plus, how am I ever going to be operational again if I'm only going three times a week?"

"You land on that leg wrong and you'll be looking at a much longer recovery."

Cruise held the position a second longer. His broad shoulders pulled back. Thick muscles contracted, forming a valley of tanned flesh for the sweat to trickle down. Dropping to the floor, he landed on his good leg while keeping his right up. Before putting any weight on his injured leg, Cruise performed a one-legged bow, then looked at her with expectant eyes, the cobalt blue boring deep into hers.

"Are you going to make me beg? What's the op?" Cruise asked.

"It's a personal favor for Jordan."

"A personal favor?"

"His niece went missing yesterday."

"Niece? He's never mentioned a niece."

"That's because he didn't know she existed until his brother called him last night."

"So what does he want you to do?"

"Poke around, put my eyes on, see if the investigation is moving in the right direction. And help it along if it isn't."

"How does he expect you to do that?"

"Investigative reporter at your service." Holding up the ID badge, she offered a wink and half smile.

Cruise returned neither. "I don't like this. Maybe I should go with you."

"I don't need a babysitter. And this isn't a tac op."

"It's always better to have more eyes on any operation. Regardless of whether it's tactical or not."

"Usually. But not in this case."

"Why's that?"

"Small towns have a lot of eyes and bigger mouths. Easier to avoid both if there's only one person." Hatch looked beneath Cruise's tough exterior and saw the disappointment in his eyes. "This is just intel and investigation. Missing persons cases are bread and butter, basics of any investigator. I should be in and out in a day or two."

"I've seen what can happen with you in a day or two."

"Jordan wants to keep this thing on the down-low on his end as well. This one's off the books. Harder to explain if both of us go off the rez." That seemed to satiate the worry in Cruise, at least for the moment. "Look, I think Jordan just wants to do his part, and help his brother."

"He's never spoken of his brother either."

"Too much history there. I'll let him fill you in if he wants."

Hatch moved to the bedroom and opened the middle drawer where she kept her stuff. She didn't own much, and she hadn't tried to accumulate many new clothes since arriving back in Cruise's life. She still wasn't sure where their relationship stood.

Looking at the bed they had shared that morning, she knew he was smart enough to know that keeping only a duffel bag's worth of stuff in his place meant she hadn't settled in. Maybe it was because she hadn't found the nerve to confront her past, so it was showing how she was able to move toward the future.

In the nearly two months since Cruise had sustained a deep puncture in his quadricep and a fractured femur, he'd been left sour and frustrated. He'd pushed himself in physical therapy in the hopes of returning to the team sooner rather than later. Hatch knew that as he watched her pack and prepare to go somewhere without him, the invisible divide between them continued to build.

She tried to soften the mood. "Most of these missing person cases turn up. The mom's involved in some cultish religious group. The girl is twelve. Maybe she got wise to it and bolted. The highest percentage of missing persons are runaways."

"And what if this isn't? What's the other percentage?" Cruise asked, using the dresser for a crutch.

"Then it's worse. That's why I have to get there quickly. On the off chance it's something more, every minute that passes is critical if Kyla's been abducted. I shouldn't be gone long. I plan to be back in time for Taylor's service at the end of the week."

The mention of Taylor sealed Cruise's lips. The crash that had taken Cruise's mobility was the same one that took the life of his teammate. Tracy may have been the commander of the op, but it was Cruise leading the team on the ground. There was no heavier burden than being responsible for a fellow operator's death, regardless of circumstance and situation.

"When are you off?" Cruise asked.

"My flight leaves in two hours."

Cruise moved in close. Placing his hands on her hips, he pulled her closer, his warm body damp with sweat pressing hard against hers. "Then what you're saying is we've got just enough time?" He flashed a wink.

"Looks like you'll have to do a few more pullups to burn off that energy." Offering a kiss instead. "I should get going."

"Raincheck." Cruise offered an exaggerated pouty frown as he released his grip on her hipline. And don't hesitate to call if you need something. I'll be there in a heartbeat."

Just then, Hatch's cell phone vibrated on the dresser near the envelope containing her new credentials. She looked at the caller ID. Dalton Savage.

Her stomach churned, and she felt her face redden. Cruise looked down at the phone as Hatch sent the call to voicemail.

"Looks like your past is catching up with you."

"Then I guess I'll have to keep moving forward."

Hatch stuffed enough clothing to last three or four days into her duffel and zipped it up. Cruise stopped her at the door to their bedroom, grabbed her and kissed her.

"I'll be here when you come back. So make sure you do."

"I haven't met a storm I couldn't weather." Hatch smiled at Cruise.

The former SEAL turned and faced the sun. Reaching skyward, he grabbed the pullup bar. Hatch looked at his rippling back and then over to her dresser drawer, now almost empty, as she shouldered her bag and headed out the door.

SEVEN

SAVAGE SAT IN THE WAITING ROOM. IT WAS STERILE. A COUPLE CHAIRS, A coffee table with an assortment of magazines, everything you expect from a doctor's office. Why should he expect anything less from a psychiatrist? Although he did notice the magazines were more geared towards wellness, yoga, and healthy lifestyle stuff. No gossip magazines, nothing that could incite or infuriate. No newspapers. The TV in the waiting area played tranquil images, and the PA system filled the area with the soft, soothing sound of rushing water and wind chimes. A serenity candle burned in the corner.

Dr. Becca Somers was renowned in her field of study and had been hired by the Graver family after they left Hawk's Landing and moved to Steamboat Springs, Colorado. The state police had kept Savage informed on the status of their investigation in the days since the shooting. Although Billy Graver had still not spoken, and his attorney had not offered up another opportunity for a conversation, they had learned that Billy Graver had spent most of his time in inpatient and outpatient mental health therapy. He spent four years at the Somers Institute, an inpatient, well-living facility for challenged youth, which made mainstream schooling a challenge. So not only was Dr. Somers a psychiatrist, but also a teacher, mentor, and parent figure to many of these children.

Savage had sought her assistance seeing that as far as clinicians went, A, she was easiest to access—the attorneys weren't surrounding and protecting her; and B, she had spent the most time with Graver. The case was open and closed. There was no question whether Graver pulled the trigger and killed Miller. Evelyn Mann stood a foot away as a witness, and there was surveillance on the grocery store's camera. But simply knowing that Graver committed the crime did not explain why he did so. For Savage, the why was his itch.

Of every homicide he'd ever worked, the only ones to haunt him were the ones where he could not answer why.

Just as he reached down and picked up a magazine cover with someone standing in a Warrior One pose, reaching up with the sunset behind them, the door opened. An attractive woman about Savage's age entered the waiting room.

Having already seen patients both in her office and on the grounds of the Somers Institute that morning, she still looked bright-eyed and bushy-tailed, as if she'd just woken up and had a bit of Jasmine's coffee. He found it funny that the moment he saw this attractive woman, he first thought of Hatch's mother and then Hatch.

This happened often, more often than he'd ever admit. Hatch was on his mind all the time, but the woman standing in front of him caught his attention. However, he wasn't here for socialization. He wasn't here to fill the void that Hatch left in his life for a second time when she left for good. He was here for answers, and the lean-built woman approaching him with her bright blue eyes and welcoming smile was his best chance.

"Sheriff Savage?"

Dalton stood. "Dalton. Dr. Somers, I presume?"

"Becca. Follow me."

They walked down a short hallway and entered her office on the left-hand side. Across the hall, he saw another closed door. Through a window, he could see it was a room designed for therapy play for younger patients.

"Have a seat. Now, I've heard the news, so I know this is a tragic time. I can't speak to Billy Graver's condition without being held liable, even though he is no longer my patient. So I would need a legal consent from the family or the family's attorney to proceed in disclosing any information to you. I don't think I can tell you much more, and I hate to waste your long drive out here."

"Driving helps clear my head. If nothing else, maybe I can come to some resolution between the here and there."

"I like that," Somers said with a genuineness that made Savage believe it. "Between the here and there. Well, I know the Gravers must be dealing with a lot, as well as the victim's family. This is a very upsetting situation, an outburst like that.

"That's what I'm getting at. All I have on Billy Graver is the story I've been told by my deputies and the research I did afterwards. A young boy, age twelve, disappears with his sister. A week later he's found alone, and there were droplets of his sister's blood on his clothes, but her body was never found."

"Well, you have the story. I've never been told more than that."

"My deputy knew of Billy and said that she believed he was on the spectrum."

"So you may have a partial diagnosis. There's more to Billy Graver than that. And I don't think he killed his sister. I don't think he did it at all."

"Is the behavior in line with someone with his condition?"

"Heavens no. Although there can be extreme behavioral outbursts with people like Billy. Nothing I've experienced or read as a clinician would support what happened in that grocery store." Somers gave a pensive look. "No. Something else was at work there. I just don't know what."

"Is there anything you can tell me about Billy that would shed any light on this case? Or maybe you could act as an intermediary in an interview setting and assist me in trying another go at the questioning?"

"As to Graver's medical information, I can only speak in generalities to the condition and not the individual. And as far as assisting in an interview, it would be a waste of time. For the most part, Billy Graver is non-communicative. Meaning he is just as likely to remain silent with me as he would you. I'm just trying to save you from spending unnecessary energy on trying to get him to talk, so you can focus your efforts in a direction that may give you the answers you seek."

"Hard to let go of the idea that trapped inside Billy's mind is the answer to what happened to his sister and the reason he opened fire on Glenn Miller."

"I can see that this case, or something else, is burdening you." Somers offered a gentle smile. "It's what I do for a living."

Savage thought about his own shooting. The one that had derailed him, the burden that he always carried with that, and wondered if Somers could see it. He looked around her room. It was painted a soft green with a yellow accent wall. Everything was warm and comforting, even the woman's demeanor. Savage wondered if maybe she could help him with his other burdens. He let the thought slip from his mind as he continued his focus. Billy Graver.

"Do you think he killed his sister?" Savage asked. "This isn't a clinical question. Just two people talking."

"No." Her voice steady. No trace of hesitation in her answer.

"Did you see the news? Miller's murder was witnessed by several bystanders and captured on the grocery's security camera. For whatever the reason, Billy Graver is a murderer. What makes you so sure he wasn't capable of killing his sister ten years before?"

"Sheriff, do you ever get a hunch and it turns out to be correct?"

"Sure. Best cops always follow their gut."

"I'd say the same is true in my line of work. The brain is referred to as gray matter. For me, its grayness is the murky depth of the mind's many secrets. I often find myself following my own gut instincts when dealing with the uniqueness of my patients."

"I guess you would know his psychology, probably better than most. Maybe even better than the doctors caring for him now."

"Well, school is part of the formative years, yes. I do get to counsel and work with these kids at a closer level and on different tasks besides just daily sessions. But I will tell you that in my four years with Billy Graver, he said very little."

"He said little. What did he say?"

"Now *that*, I cannot say."

"Well, could I tell you what I know and maybe you could tell me if where I'm going may be right?"

"We could try it."

"That's the point. I had seen something like this when I was with homicide in Denver, a similar case. A killing that seemed uncharacteristic for the quiet, unassuming boy. Turned out he was attacking his alleged abuser. Billy Graver is much like a timepiece, but something caused him to work his way back and find Miller. I haven't figured out how he got from here back to Hawk's Landing not being able to communicate."

"Well, just because he doesn't speak doesn't mean he can't use a computer, order some tickets, and get to where he needs to go." Somers said.

"He was able to acquire a gun and use it to kill somebody, so his resourcefulness has nothing to do with his communication. There was a witness." Somers keyed in on this as Savage spoke. "She heard him saying something, and I guess that's what's nagging me. I didn't want to say it over the phone because I don't like to speak about active investigations, just like you don't speak about your patients."

Somers gave a half smile and a nod. "All right, I'll bite."

"Okay." Savage wanted to barter, a tit-for-tat, but felt that whatever Somers's image, she would respect his honesty and maybe offer something of an answer in turn. A witness heard him say something. He was still mouthing it when we got to him, but at a distance and my commands and the tension, I didn't hear it. The witness thought he was saying, 'Protect him.' Mean anything to you?"

Somers sat back for a minute. Her face first looked as though it didn't make sense, but then her eyes widened. "You're saying that Billy was saying, 'Protect him.' He wasn't saying that."

The psychologist reached across her desk and pulled a small set of keys from underneath a stack of papers. She used one of the keys to unlock the oak cabinet behind her. She rifled through its interior. A few seconds later, she held an old composition notebook.

On the cover, written in very neat handwriting on the "Belonged to" tag, "William Graver, age 14," with a date range underneath it that Savage couldn't see. "I shouldn't show you this, and I'll never say that I did." Somers passed the notebook to Savage.

Savage opened the book and flipped about two-thirds of the way through it. The pages were rippled with hard-pressed lines from a dark pen. It felt like braille. He looked down at the scribble and swirls, some letters shaped hardline, some round, some small, some big, the words forming overlapping figure eights, and all saying the same thing.

Dr. Somers was right. He wasn't saying, "Protect him." He was saying, "Prodigium."

"Prodigium? What does that mean?" Savage asked.

"It's Latin for monster."

EIGHT

Hatch had used the six hours of travel to commit the details, what little she had at this point, to memory. She also fleshed out the narrative of her cover story, mentally rehearsing the answers to the likely questions that may arise once in town. The best lies were born in truth. Covers were just a lie by another name.

During the first leg of her travel, she'd had the entire row to herself. But she wasn't as lucky after changing planes at George Bush Intercontinental Airport in Houston.

The two had shared their three-seat row by the wing of the plane and the emergency exit to Hatch's left provided her row with extra foot room. The seat between them had been vacant, although the large man in the aisle seat occupied a portion of it, having lifted the armrest to allow his ample girth to spill out from his own seat. He hadn't been much for talking when he boarded, which Hatch had been ok with. And the nipper of spiced rum he'd added to his Coke had aided in putting the man to sleep before the wheels had lifted off in Texas.

Hatch's flight touched down at Nashville International Airport just as the Tennessee sun was setting. The interior cabin was ablaze in the dazzling magenta hue of its glow. The tires of the plane bumped and skipped, jostling the small tablet in Hatch's hand. She found her place and continued to reread the short article Tracy had forwarded her. Just as he said, there wasn't much there.

The newspaper column was only five short paragraphs. The Shepherd was quoted only once, saying, "I was called here. And my flock followed." There was mention that The Shepherd refused to answer a question about how he came to purchase three hundred acres of land for a man who claimed to have no ties to the outside world.

The man sharing Hatch's row awoke with a jolt as the plane taxied along the runway. Hatch hoped he would pull out his phone and ignore her like most of the other passengers on the plane were doing. He turned to Hatch and smiled. She could see he was the type to seize opportunities like this to make idle chit chat, that thing travelers do to ease the awkwardness in the last few minutes of sharing a close space with a total stranger.

He twisted in his seat and extended a big hand in Hatch's direction. She politely—if not reluctantly—accepted. Shaking his hand in the awkward position had pulled Hatch's right sleeve up above her wrist, exposing the tail end of the twisted scar that ran her entire arm up to her right shoulder. Hatch figured now to be as good a time as any to take her alias and backstory for a little test drive.

"Jack Burnside. My friends call me JB."

"My friends call me Hatch."

"That's a mean scar. Fire?" JB's eyes darted towards Hatch's exposed wrist.

She tugged the sleeve down. "Something like that."

"Military?"

Hatch answered with a nod of her head, mixing the truth of her past into her cover, remembering to keep it vague enough.

This pleased Burnside, and a smile widened on his face. "Me, too. Long ago. Two tours in 'Nam. Feels like a lifetime ago, but some days it feels like yesterday. Don't know if that makes any sense?"

"It does. Hatch knew the truth in Burnside's words better than she'd care to admit. There were moments where she felt she was back in that moment. Sometimes when her mind jerked her back in time, Hatch let it play out differently. In this alternate reality, she didn't hesitate. Instead, she fired her kill shot in that split-second interval before the little girl appeared from behind her mother's dress. In those rewrites of her memory, the bomb never detonated. Graham Benson, former Task Force Banshee member and friend, would still be alive to see his little daughter grow up. But the alternate universe never lasted. The scar along her arm served as a permanent anchor to her reality.

"You deploy?" Burnside asked.

"A couple times."

"War is all the same."

"How's that?"

"It all comes down to the guy in the foxhole next to you."

"Or girl," Hatch flashed a smile.

"Brave new world. You still in the service?"

"No." Hatch gestured to the tablet and fished out the reporter badge from her pocket. "I traded my rifle for a pen."

"Is it true what they say?"

"About what?"

"That the pen is truly mightier than the sword?"

"Sometimes." Hatch thought of Miguel Ayala, the reporter from Juarez, Mexico, who had shown her the truest meaning of bravery and the power of the human spirit.

"You heading to Nashville on business?"

Hatch felt now was as good and safe a time as any to practice her backstory. "I live here. Well, I do now. I was visiting a friend in California."

"I see. How long have you been in the area?"

"Little less than a year. Still getting my foothold."

"How do you like it?"

"It's been great so far. I can't really complain."

"So, less than a year. Were you here for the big one?"

Hatch had read up on the area and found several references to a devastating series of tornadoes in March 2020.

"No, I got here a few months after. Caught the rebuild. Devastating."

"I live east of here, away from the city up in Mt. Juliet. My house got torn up real good. Those nasty twisters stripped it down to the foundation."

"That must've been tough."

"My family wasn't home. Kids are grown and off tackling the world. My wife passed years back. Just me and my lonesome. Took to my shelter, everybody with half a brain around here has one, and rode it out." Burnside shrugged. "But I lived through it, and houses can always be rebuilt. Not so easy with people."

Hatch thought of the fire that nearly took her family's life. It still wasn't lost on her the irony of now working with the agency responsible.

"The contractors just finished the remodel. Stayed at my brother's house in San Diego while it was under construction." He shook his head and chuckled to himself. "Got the damn thing rebuilt just in time to see another end to tornado season."

"How long's it last? The tornado season." Hatch asked.

"Things are at worst February through April, but November can be a bit dicey too. Each season is different. Some knock the snot out of this state, like last year's. Others not so much. This year's been pretty timid. Fingers crossed it stays that way."

The stewardess walked by, and Burnside plucked the empty nipper out of the seat pocket in front of him and tossed it in the trash bag. The stewardess gave a knowing look. Burnside's cheeks reddened as he offered a playful wink in return before she moved on to the next row.

"So, any big stories you're working on?" Burnside turned his attention back to Hatch.

"I'm doing a piece on the Eternal Light."

Burnside grumbled.

"You've heard of them?"

"Don't know much. But I do business in Jericho Falls from time to time. I know they're a bunch of crazies and halfwits. They follow that lunatic preacher, calls himself The Shepherd. Walks around like some kind of prophet. Reminds me of those Branch Davidians out in Waco years back. "

"Have any dealings with them?"

"Is what I say going in your story?"

"I never know until I know."

Burnside gave a slow nod. "I haven't had much to do with 'em, but they meander about town from time to time. Ever since he showed up in the area with those tunic-wearing nut jobs, I feel like they've been nothing but trouble."

"Trouble is what I do best."

The captain announced their arrival at the gate. For a large man, Burnside made quick work of getting out of his seat and into the aisle. They exchanged well wishes. As they departed the gangway, Hatch bypassed the baggage claim. She'd taken her duffel as a carry-on.

Hatch picked up the Jeep Grand Cherokee from the rental company and began making the forty-minute drive east to Jericho Falls. The last rays of light silhouetted the Nashville skyline as she drove toward the impending darkness.

NINE

SAVAGE DECIDED NOT TO CALL BEFORE STOPPING BY THE HOUSE. A LIGHT rain began to fall as he stood outside. Knocking at the door, he waited. He heard movement from inside that sounded like a chair creaking, soft footsteps, and then the lock turning. The door opened a crack and half the face of an old woman peered at him through wire-rimmed glasses. She looked like she could've been cast in a Grandma's Cookies advertisement. There was a sweetness to her, hidden behind timid eyes. A dark sadness hung over her like a storm cloud, as she welcomed Savage in, her voice hollow and her eyes vacant.

The state police had done a good job of keeping the media away from Glenn Miller's wife, Sue. Undoubtedly, however, she had seen the countless broadcasts and endless 24-hour news stations loop, re-sensationalizing the event as any little breadcrumb dropped from the state police's public affairs officer. She saw Savage's badge first and then recognized his face.

On many occasions passing through town he had met Sue Miller, but never had much of a conversation. Just friendly waves.

"Oh, Sheriff. I'm sorry, I didn't realize it was you. There's been a revolving door of men with badges since—" She let the sentence trail off. Her tired eyes met his. "I just put on the kettle for some tea if you'd like."

He tapped the thermos in his hand that contained his daily batch of Jasmine's special brew. There was a hint of cinnamon today. "I'm all set for now, but thanks for the offer, Mrs. Miller."

"Sue's fine. Please, Sheriff, won't you come on in."

Savage followed the widow inside, taking off the Stetson he wore as he crossed the threshold. He spotted an open peg on the nearby coat rack, conveniently available.

The kettle whistled from the kitchen just beyond the quaint living room space in the modest ranch style house. "Well, if you don't mind, I'll be getting myself that cup of tea."

"I won't take much of your time. I just—"

She gestured for Savage to have a seat at a small table in the kitchen. A moment later, with the tea bag steeping in a mug, Sue Miller took the chair across from him. Her eyes were still damp with tears. She was sad and broken. Savage recognized both immediately, something he'd seen time and again in countless other victims over the years, and sometimes in his own mirrored reflection.

"I'm just here to clear up loose ends on the Hawk's Landing side of the case. The state police are running the investigation and have already questioned you, but I'd like to follow up. I know that this is an extremely difficult time. "

"If you're going to ask me why that abomination killed my Glenn, I'll tell you what I told them. I don't know." Anger peeked out from the darkness shrouding her like a cloak. "Glenn helped children for a living. Problematic children, like that Billy Graver." Her voice grew quieter as the embers of rage surrendered to the sadness. "I don't understand. Why?"

"That's why I'm here, Sue. This is what I'm trying to figure out."

"I remember what happened to that boy's sister, Amanda. Horrible story. First, the disappearance put everybody on edge. Then, the tragedy. I remember seeing Billy's picture in the newspaper after he was found a week later, covered in his sister's blood. They never recovered the girl's body, and Billy hasn't spoken about it since. But everybody knows what happened."

"And what is it that everybody believes happened?"

"Billy Graver killed his sister just like he killed my Glenn."

"And you believe this to be the truth?" Savage asked.

"Oh, I don't believe. I know." Sue Miller took a sip of her tea and stiffened her back. "Billy killed her."

"And how do you know this?"

"Because Glenn was his psychologist, and he told me so. Now, I know what you're thinking. Glenn shouldn't be talking about his clients. Patient-doctor privileges and all that HIPPA stuff. But working with Billy really had an impact on my husband."

"How so?"

"As soon as he took him on as a patient, Glenn became obsessed. He claimed he could truly heal the boy. I've never seen him like that, not in the years prior, nor after."

"I read your husband testified in a hearing that resulted in Billy Graver being sent to a mental hospital in Denver. Did he say anything specific about Billy?"

"He said he should've realized that Billy was unteachable."

"Unteachable? Don't you mean unreachable? Right?"

"No. I meant what I said. Glenn looked at his therapy sessions more as lessons in how to train the brain. He always thought of himself as more a mentor or guide than a counselor."

Savage was quiet for a moment. "How long were you two married?"

"Not long enough." She sighed. "We came into each other's lives late. I was born and raised right here in Hawk's Landing. But my husband didn't move into town until a little over ten years ago. "

"Where did he live before coming here?"

"Glenn lived a life before ours. He kept those two worlds separate and never talked about anything before us. As if he materialized out of thin air."

"Did you find that odd, the fact that he didn't discuss his past with you?"

"Everybody's got skeletons in their closet. I'm sure you have some of your own. As do I." She shrugged. "But if I'm being honest. At first it bothered me. But I figured he'd talk about it if he wanted. He never did, and my curiosity faded. We built our life together by focusing less on the past and more on the present."

Savage noticed a long walking staff set against the wall near the rack where he'd hung his hat. The wood was etched from top to bottom in an overlapping series of serpentine figure eights of varying sizes. "Are you a hiker?"

"Me? Gosh no." She dunked the tea bag up and down and then squeezed the tea pouch against the spoon, draining the remnants into her cup. Sue Miller stirred in a spoonful of honey and added a dash of milk before taking a sip. She followed Savage's gaze over to the walking stick. "Oh that. It was Glenn's. The only thing he brought with him from his past."

"Did it hold sentimental value for your husband?"

She nodded. "I'm afraid, like his past, Glenn never spoke of it. When I first asked him about it, he said, every good shepherd needs a staff." Her face was partially hidden by the mug she held, both hands clasped tight around the porcelain. "I guess that's how my husband saw himself. A shepherd to the lost sheep he saved during those countless hours of counseling he provided the broken souls who sought his wisdom."

Savage scanned the room, looking for any other clue that might shed light on the truth about Glenn Miller and the cause of the deadly rampage by his former patient. Looking into the quaint family room, he noticed a fishing rod above the fireplace with a large bass on display above it on a placard. "Was Mr. Miller a fisherman?"

"Oh, that thing? Funny story on that." Sue Miller's face brightened. "Glenn picked that up at the local thrift store, some unwanted hand-me-down, I guess. Bought it for two dollars and that ugly thing went up above our mantle."

"What about the rod and reel?"

"Sure, used it. Every day, in fact. Glenn would take that fishing rod out with him every morning at sunrise." She chuckled softly to herself as if somebody had whispered a joke in her ear meant only for her. "You know, he's never caught a fish? None that I ever saw at least."

"Did he take you with him?"

"No. Not once." Finishing the last bit of tea, she set the mug on the plate. "I never felt it was my place to go, anyway. Come to think of it, he picked up the fishing rod right after the Graver boy killed his sister. Her death really impacted him. I think he blamed himself for failing to reach the boy." A tear fell from Sue Miller's eyes and she wiped at it. The drop rolled down her cheek and dropped into her empty teacup.

"Thank you for your time. I know this has been hard. I just needed a snapshot into your husband's life to see if there were any dots to connect."

"And did I help?"

"More than you know. If you haven't shared this information with the state police, then I'll take care of it."

Savage stood, and Sue rose with him. "Please don't bother." Savage said. "I'll let myself out. If you think of anything else, or if there's anything I can do for you, you know how to reach me."

"Thank you for stopping by. It was nice to get a chance to talk about my Glenn with you."

Savage went to the door. Picking up his hat, he then looked over at the rod. "Do you mind telling me where his fishing hole was? Hard to find from here?"

"Impossible not to find. He walked that trail so much, it's worn down. When you get off the porch, just bend left. Look for the break in the trees, and the path is just beyond."

"Thanks again, and however this turns out, I think it's important you talk to somebody. These things can be hard. Trust me, I know." At that moment, Savage thought of Somers and he thought it odd. Usually at these times, he thought of Hatch.

THE LIGHT RAIN had increased to a torrential downpour. In a rain parka, Savage overlooked the dig site where a state police forensics team worked around Glenn Miller's fishing hole.

It hadn't taken long to secure a search and seizure warrant for the grounds. Although a slow and daunting process, Savage didn't want to leave, even though he'd been given the opportunity to dry off and warm-up in the command center RV parked about a mile away.

The area they were working in was covered by a tent, but it didn't stop all the rain rolling downhill, turning a lot of their grid work into mud. Rain was every homicide cop's enemy. The natural washing eradicated much of the evidence, and he was worried that would be the case today, but the difference was, they were excavating, and the water had turned the dirt into mud.

They'd been at it for close to six hours and were reaching a point where darkness would cause them to break, at least while they set up the lights.

Sinclair arrived with a thermos of coffee, not Jasmine Hatch's, of course, but anything warm would be welcomed.

"Sheriff, thought you might need this." She handed over a thermos.

"You didn't have to go to the trouble of making me coffee."

"I didn't. Jasmine Hatch called into the station. When I told her you were out there in the rain watching the scene, she brought this by for you. Said there's more for you back at the house if you need."

Savage tipped his hat, took the thermos, and took a grateful gulp of the hot coffee. As the warm liquid made its way down the back of his throat, it worked to alleviate some of the cold that had risen through his bones. The rain continued to patter against the thin waterproof hood.

"Sheriff, don't you think you should take a break? Could be weeks."

"Yeah, I know. But I just like to see the first day's work complete. Gives me something, a bit of satisfaction. I don't know. It's always good to take a moment and take in your scene. Remember that Becky, because this won't be your last."

A sad statement. Even in small town Hawk's Landing, Savage knew it was only a matter of time until another body would fall. No place on earth could escape the evil of some men's hearts. Wind caught up-river and sent an icy blast of cold rain into Savage's face. He turned away as the last tendrils of light gripped the sky before fading.

"I guess that's it," he said to Sinclair, taking another long pull from the thermos. "First day in the books. Maybe tomorrow will bring something else." He was turning back towards his suburban when he heard a voice call out from one of the crime scene techs.

"I found something. It's human."

Savage turned and hurried to the edge of the excavation site, not crossing the "do not cross" tape. Even as a sheriff, he couldn't access that without signing in through the proper channels.

He impatiently waited for more details from the Tyvek suit-wearing technician squatted in a hunch over section C37—three rows across, thirty-seven squares away. The photographer went over and began snapping shots of the section, getting different angles, different proximity, different levels of zoom and flash, compensating for the darkness and the falling rain.

Slowly, bit by bit, the remains were removed after being photographed in place. Buried in the ground beside the small skeletal frame was a friendship bracelet with colorful trinkets and lettered beads that spelled, "Mandy."

TEN

Rain began to fall, then subsequently tapered off as Hatch exited I-40 following the signs south to Jericho Falls. The lights on the highway were lost among the trees. Ten minutes later, she passed a wooden sign that said, "Jericho Falls, Population 1,236." Smaller than Hawk's Landing. But Hatch knew better than most the secrets that a small town could hold. The trajectory her life had taken since her homecoming after running from her past for fifteen years had put her on the path she was on now, the one that brought her here.

Hatch followed her phone's GPS to the only inn within twenty miles of the town. Turning off the main road, she followed a winding path lined with trees. The motel sat on a low hill.

The motel itself was a strip of eight rows with an oversized parking lot, ideal for 18-wheelers taking respite from their long haul. Aside from the black Ford pickup parked in front of the office, there were no other vehicles in the lot.

Her Jeep's tires crackled and popped over the lot's crushed stone surface. She pulled to a stop next to the truck, got out, and went inside the motel office. The door chimed as she entered, and she heard a man grunt from the room behind the main desk.

She heard the scrape of a chair, and a moment later, a man wearing a trucker cap and a denim shirt with the nametag "Harlin" above his left breast pocket approached from the other side of the counter. Eying Hatch he gave a tip of his cap.

"How can I help you this evening?"

"Looking for a room."

He looked back at the rack of keys. Every room key hung from their hook with their respective room number above. The key to room one was missing. Harlin grabbed the key for room three and set it on the counter between them.

"How long you plannin' on stayin'?"

"Depends." Hatch offered a shrug. "Definitely tonight. I'll have to see after that."

He was quiet for a moment as he sized her up. She knew the look, having seen it before. Hatch was an outsider. Harlin, being the only motel manager within twenty miles of the town, served as a gate-keeper of sorts, giving him first look at any visitors.

He gave a barely noticeable nod of his head, Hatch having passed whatever silent evaluation he'd given, and said, "It's sixty for the night. I'm going to need a driver's license and credit card. You won't be charged until you check out."

Hatch laid the license Jordan Tracy had made for her on the coun-tertop. Harlin picked it up and then looked up at Hatch.

"You only live forty minutes away from here. Why do you need to put up in my motel?" His guardedness returned in the tone with which he asked the question.

Hatch produced the other ID, the one showing her employment as an investigative reporter with The Blaze.

"A reporter, eh? Working on anything big?" Harlin asked, dropping the judgement from his voice.

"Never know until I get there."

"Don't know there's much to say about our quiet old town. What're you plannin' to write about here in little ole Jericho Falls?"

"I'm doing a story on the Eternal Light."

"I was wondering when those dress-wearing holy rollers would get themselves the attention of the media. Only a matter of time, I guess."

"And why's that?" Hatch asked.

"Because, to put it bluntly, they're just plain strange."

"Strange how?"

"Well, you're smack dab in the Bible belt. People round here love themselves some Jesus. They sure do." Harlin paused to slip a tooth-pick into the corner of his mouth, toggling the small splinter of wood into position with his tongue. "They wear those long dress-like clothes, handmade sandals, the works."

"And that bothers you?"

"I'm as much a believer as the next guy. Just don't see no need to go flauntin' it around." He flicked the toothpick to the other side of his mouth. "Guess it just rubs me the wrong way. But don't go gettin' me wrong. I'm not saying they're bad. Just is, they're different. And around here, sometimes that's one and the same. If you catch my drift?"

"Have you had much in the way of interaction, personally, with them?"

"As much as anybody, I guess. No doubt you'll see them around town, but I wouldn't bother tryin' to interview them for your story."

"Why is that?"

"They don't take kindly to outsiders or even to us townsfolk asking about their business. Heck, I'm pretty sure they consider us outsiders. And I've lived here my entire life."

"What's your take on them?"

Harlin started shaking his head from side to side before speaking, took a step back, and raised both hands.

"No ma'am. You're not going to get me quoted in no paper, no how. Won't catch me being the town gossip."

"I don't cite my sources to anyone. Ever."

"Be that as it may, I am a good Christian man and I do not like to speak about other people who are not in my presence."

Hatch opened her mouth to speak.

"But," Harlin continued. "I will tell you this. I've got no problem with them, personally. In my opinion, I think this world needs more God-fearing folk. I don't see them doing no harm. Heck, when those tornadoes ripped through here last year, half the town got torn up."

"I wasn't in Nashville then, but I heard it was pretty bad." Hatch using what she'd gathered from JB during the final few minutes of her flight.

"But when the winds died down, it was The Shepherd and his flock who showed up the morning after to help rebuild. Part of my gosh dang roof got ripped off during that storm that caught us off-guard in the first week of March. And you know who fixed it? They did. The whole bunch came through town, even the young'uns helped in any way they could. Rebuilt my roof and asked for nothing in return."

"They wouldn't accept any money?"

"Not their way. They believe in service as the reward." The motel owner shrugged. "Good people, doing God's work, I guess. Good doesn't come at a price. At least, that's what the preacher said."

"The little I read about the Eternal Light and their preacher didn't mention the name of their Shepherd. You wouldn't happen to know it offhand, would you?"

"Nope. Far as I know, nobody here does. His followers don't use their legal names either. They go by names like Sunbeam. Reminds me of the 70s. Bunch of peace-lovin' hippies with a healthy dose of Jesus." Harlin leveled his gaze at her. "You got yourself some religion?"

Hatch answered as honestly as she could. "My conversation with God runs more like a debate. There have been moments in my life that gave me pause to question that relationship."

"We're all tested by the Lord in different ways." Harlin eyed the scar poking out from her right sleeve. "It's sometimes hard to see the wisdom in His design. But trust me, it's there. So, whatever your story is, Ms. Hatch, I'd advise you to make sure you know the good they've done."

"I'm as open minded as they come. When I do a story, I remain objective."

"Any time someone puts their mind to something, objectivity becomes irrelevant."

"I couldn't find their community on the map. Where are they located exactly?"

"Like I said, they keep pretty much to themselves. But it's no secret. I can give you directions, but I wouldn't make a point of trying to go after dark."

"Why is that?"

"They don't like visitors, especially unannounced ones, and especially at night. You won't find yourself welcome. If you plan to visit, I recommend goin' in the morning. The gate opens at sunrise and closes at sunset. Visitors are welcome during those times."

Good to know. Hatch looked outside at the darkened parking lot. There were still plenty of hours between now and tomorrow's sunrise.

Harlin continued. "Now, if you are planning to head out that way, you're going to go back down the hill and head into the town center. Follow Main Street for about three miles outside the last light of town. You'll pass a red mailbox. Now, that's Clem Johnson's place. He lives next door if there's such a thing out here. Well, if you're snooping around, he won't be there either. Clem runs the only restaurant in town, and he's there from before sun-up and stays long after dark. After Clem's house, follow that road for about another two, maybe three miles. You'll see some large wooden crosses on the side of the road. The dirt trail that leads in runs about a quarter mile long, at the end of which you'll run into the main gate to the property."

"Thanks."

Hatch reached into her wallet and pulled out some cash. "About that payment. How about we make it eighty bucks a night, and we do it by cash? I'll pay each day as I go."

Harlin looked at the money and then cocked an eye at Hatch.

"I like to keep things off the books. It helps with protecting my story and my sources." Hatch said.

"I can respect that."

Hatch put the money on the counter and picked up the key and her ID. Harlin handed Hatch a twenty back.

"No need for the extra twenty. I'm an honest man."

"Thanks for taking the time to talk to me, and what you said, I'll keep in confidence."

Harlin gave another tip of his hat. "Unless you plan on dining from the limited selection of my vending machine, I'd head down to Clem's before he closes if you want a hot meal tonight."

Hatch put her room key in her pocket.

"I just might take you up on that," she said, as she walked out the door.

ELEVEN

SAVAGE SAT IN A SMALL ROOM NOT UNLIKE THAT OF HIS OWN interrogation room. But he was the one waiting in the room alone this time, and just like his own interrogation room, there were no windows and no clocks. The Colorado Mental Health Institute in Pueblo housed those deemed criminally insane. Since Graver's shooting, the care facility had served as his temporary living quarters.

In the swirl of investigative fury following the discovery of Amanda's remains, Savage had levied to have the State Police shift their prosecutorial efforts, citing the unknown trauma experienced during Billy Graver's captivity during the blizzard ten years ago as the catalyst for the shooting death of Glenn Miller.

The state prosecutor, after some pressure from a mental health advisory board headed by Dr. Becca Somers, yielded and opted for long-term psychological treatment as the alternative approach to prosecution. Because of her extensive work and established rapport, built over several years of therapy, Somers was also assigned as his primary clinician and would resume her work with Graver once the dust settled on the case.

As if by some cosmic intuitive force, Savage's cellphone vibrated on the table in front of him. The incoming message was from Somers.

It read, I really appreciate all you've done for Billy and his family. I enjoyed our conversation during our brief meeting. I'd like to keep the dialogue going with you. Maybe the next time we meet up, it could be over a cup of coffee or glass of wine.

He read the message a second time before he noticed Sinclair peeking over his shoulder. Slipping the phone back in his pocket, he thought about Somers's text. And then he thought about Hatch, and the lack thereof. For the first time since Hatch had disappeared from his life, Savage wondered if maybe his chance at happiness could be found elsewhere.

"I can't believe we had it wrong all those years." Sinclair sat beside Savage and nervously clicked the back of her pen.

"It's an unfortunate set of circumstances, that's for sure. No way anyone could've predicted the outcome."

"Ten years is a long time to silently hold on to whatever happened to him and his sister in that mountain cave."

"I'm not sure he'll ever be able to tell the tale." Savage thought of the crime scene where they'd arrested Graver. Then he recalled the image of the bullet riddled body of Glenn Miller. "But he spoke louder than any words could when he pulled the trigger."

"Now I understand your need for closure on this, but do you really think it's going to do any good?" Sinclair stopped the repetitive clicking and set the pen aside. "Billy doesn't speak."

"But he listens. And today, that's all I need him to do." Savage sat up as he heard footsteps approach from the other side of the door.

A large friendly faced orderly with a nametag that read Briggs had escorted Savage into the room after Savage had gained the Gravers' permission to visit with Billy. Briggs now escorted Graver in. Savage realized upon seeing the orderly in the white button-down shirt and white slacks that this was the same outfit he had seen Billy Graver in when he'd executed seventy-two-year-old Glenn Miller. The monster.

Graver didn't look at Savage. The orderly clicked twice and in a robotic manner, Graver took his seat, his hands placed evenly on the table just as they had been when in shackles in Savage's custody. He looked past Savage at the wall behind him and the tapping continued like actual clockwork. Savage knew without looking at his watch that Billy Graver was keeping the time.

"Billy, I have approval from your family to speak with you. I don't know if you can hear me, but I hope you can. I spoke with Dr. Somers. She spoke well of you, and she said you're very intelligent." The tapping continued, the eyes still looking beyond Savage. "I know why you did it, why you shot Glenn Miller. He took your sister, Amanda." The tapping continued.

Tap, tap, tap.

"I can't say I wouldn't have done the same thing."

Tap, tap, tap.

Savage took an envelope from a leather briefcase by the foot of his chair and slid it across the table to Graver.

Tap, tap, tap.

Keeping his eyes straight ahead, he didn't look down at the object in his hands.

"It's okay, Billy."

Tap, tap, tap.

Savage stood from his chair, reached across the table, and opened the envelope, sliding the contents of it onto the table. The bracelet rattled, and it touched Graver's index finger as it settled down. He didn't tap again. His finger rested on the M. His eyes broke contact with the wall and he looked down. His body remained rigid, but a single tear fell from his eye and splashed down on the table near his sister's bracelet.

"The monster's gone, Billy. You got him. Your sister is at peace now."

Savage knew it would only provide a part of the peace he could never seek. The horrible crimes human beings are capable of, and the things left in the wake leave a watermark. Savage thought about his own watermarks. Then he thought of Becca Somers and wondered if she could provide him with a peace, one he'd long sought but seldom found, not just in the trauma of his own past but in the unforeseen road ahead.

TWELVE

HATCH TOSSED HER DUFFEL ONTO THE BED IN HER ROOM. WHAT THE motel lacked in amenities was made up for by the cleanliness of the small space. Returning to her Jeep, she headed out of the gravel lot back into town.

She followed Harlin's directions. Just as he had described, after nearly two miles of a dark road stretching past the town's Main Street, she came upon the red mailbox belonging to Clem Johnson.

Continuing down the road, keeping an eye on the dash, she noted the distance traveled. She slowed as she reached the two-mile mark and scanned the roadside for the path to the Eternal Light community. And just as Harlin had said, right between the two- and three-mile marks—2.7 miles to be exact—was the dirt path that broke off to the right of the road.

It was shrouded on both sides by a thick cluster of trees. There were no lights, no signs, no mailboxes. Nothing but the path.

Hatch turned off the main road and headed in. The road stretched straight ahead, then bent slightly to the right. As she rounded the bend, the headlights of the Jeep illuminated the ten-foot-high wooden fence with an arched gateway big enough for a truck to pass through.

Hatch stopped ten feet from the gate. Cutting the engine, she stepped out of her Jeep. Pushing the door shut gently, so the sound was nothing more than a click, she stood by the car for a moment, adjusting herself to the darkness and her surroundings. A lyrical hum could be heard from the other side of the walls, just beyond the wind rattling the leaves.

Hatch walked to the main gate. There was a slight gap between the gate and the fence post. She was able to catch a glimpse of the compound's interior. A bright orange campfire illuminated the circle of faces surrounding it, all adorned in long, white robes.

The sounds became clearer, though the words were muffled by the wind. They were singing, and one member of the circle strummed a guitar in tune. Hatch was straining to see more when the cell phone in her pocket vibrated.

She pulled it out, saw the caller ID was Savage and sent it to voice-mail. As she re-pocketed the phone, the fire-light cast between the slit disappeared when a dark form filled the void. Hatch heard a strange grunting sound from the other side of the fence, but in the darkness couldn't make out any of the features of the person standing before her.

Hatch then pulled her reporter ID badge out and held it to the gap, up towards the tall shadowy form's head. "I'm with The Blaze. I'd like to speak with the preacher."

The man on the other side made the same grumbling, grunting noise again, but said no words. A small slip of paper held by dirt-covered fingernails came through the crack. Hatch took the note.

There was one word on it. "Leave."

Not wanting to press her luck and negotiate with the silent grunting man any further, she took Harlin's words into account and decided to leave until morning.

"Please tell the preacher that I'd like to speak to him, and I'll be back in the morning to do so."

Hatch walked back towards her Jeep. She looked back as she opened the door. The dark shadow between the gate and the post remained. In the distance, just beyond the bend in the road, she saw a small orange flicker. It took her a moment for her eyes to focus through the dark.

The orange dimmed and then grew bright again, and she recognized it. Somebody was smoking a cigarette. The moonlight provided enough light through the canopy for Hatch to just make out the shape of a small four-door sedan.

Hatch got into her car and as she started the ignition, she saw the brake lights in her rearview mirror. It backed out fast, spinning tires against the dirt. Hatch reversed and made a quick K-turn, but by the time she rounded the bend, the sedan was gone.

Hatch drove the quarter mile stretch back to the main road as fast as the path allowed. Through the thick trees, she hadn't been able to see which direction the car had gone. Hatch sped back the five miles but saw no sign of the sedan. At the town center, she saw the hand-painted sign outside the diner that read, "Clem's," and decided to stop in for a bite to eat.

HATCH PARKED in front of the diner. The building had a long front porch attached to it with a three-step walk up, the boards of which creaked loudly as she made her way to the door. Hatch entered as a gust of wind kicked up out of nowhere and slammed the door behind her, causing several of the patrons to startle and look up from their meals.

An older black man with thick cheeks, a wire-thin white mustache, and a well-groomed head of hair to match, was wiping down the counter. He looked up and gave Hatch a nod and went back about his business. Hatch made her way over and took a seat in a booth.

"Sorry about the slam to your door. That wind came out of nowhere."

"The wind around here is no joking matter. It'll sneak up and snatch your life if you're not careful. A cup of coffee while you look at the menu? Just made a fresh pot."

"Coffee sounds great. Thanks."

Setting the mug in front of her, he filled it up. "Just passing through?"

Hatch set down a notepad in front of her, alongside her ID badge and pen. "I'm on assignment. I stay as long as the story calls for."

"Here? In little old Jericho Falls? You've got to be kidding me!"

"I go where they send me."

"So, what's the story?"

"The Eternal Light."

"What kind of story?"

"An editorial piece. They came up on my editor's horizon and he sent me to check them out, see if there is a story there." Hatch stirred in some sugar and a dash of cream and took a sip. "You wouldn't happen to be Clem Johnson by any chance?"

"I am indeed."

"And you're the closest neighbor?"

The restaurant owner folded his arms across his stained apron. "Let me guess. You're staying up at the motel."

"Yes, I am."

"That Harlin Gessup. Might as well change his name to Harlin Gossip the way he talks about folk."

"He didn't say much, and I did all the asking. It's my job."

"Well, my job is keeping people well fed. Are you hungry?"

"What's good?"

"I've got a mean shepherd's pie, just out of the oven."

"Then that's what I'll have."

Johnson disappeared into the kitchen and reappeared a moment later with a plate. The layers of mashed potato, beef, mushrooms, and corn covered the surface, and a small piece of cornbread was tucked on the side.

"Now, you've got to try my cornbread. I make it every day from scratch."

Hatch took a bite. It was the perfect balance of moist and sweet. It almost melted in her mouth.

"In all the places I've traveled, that by far is the best cornbread I've ever had."

Hatch meant it, but she also knew that the key strategy to any successful interview or interrogation was building rapport, connecting with people on a personal level.

The breaking of bread seemed to ease Clem. His arms were no longer folded, and he poured a cup of coffee for himself.

"Make sure you mention that in your article. Maybe you'll get a couple more people through this way."

"Will do. How long you been in Jericho Falls?" Hatch asked, as she readied the cornbread for another bite.

"Been here my whole life. Always planned on joining the Army and seeing the world the way my father had. He was an old World War II grunt. It wasn't the stories of war that fascinated me but the places he'd seen, places as a child I could only imagine."

"Did you join?"

"Never got the chance. My father died when I was seventeen. I took over running the restaurant, keeping business alive for my mother, and every time I wanted to leave, it just couldn't happen. So, now I get to see the world through the stories of the travelers who pass through. I'm sure in your profession, you've seen plenty. Maybe we'll share a story or two ourselves while you're here."

"I'd like that," Hatch said. "If you don't mind me asking, what can you tell me about the Eternal Light?"

He looked at the pad and pen next to the plate of shepherd's pie. "Not much to tell, really. I don't have anything to do with them. A neighbor is a loose statement. Fact, our properties are adjoining, but that's about it. There's a couple miles between my home and where they all live. But they keep to themselves. You'll see them in town now and again. They help out when things go bad, don't ask for much in return. It's a strange relationship that's grown over the years. I remember when they first came into town."

"How long ago was that?"

"Had to be twenty years, maybe. Lot of folk were scared of them then, but in time, they saw they had no reason to be. We've been in a peaceful coexistence for as long as I can remember. They live by a different set of rules. Their preacher interprets the word of God the way he sees fit, and his people follow it. I don't agree with it, but I don't judge. They've got their fence secluding them from the rest of the world. They don't like trespassers, that's for sure. But there's a small waterfall, about ten, fifteen feet high in the middle of their property. Extends into a stream that crosses onto my property. Their fence is pretty much complete, except for that little patch where the river flows through. From time to time I catch the kids wandering onto my property. Don't matter where you come from, kids will always be kids, I guess."

"That much is true. I wanted to ask if you heard about the missing girl?"

Clem nodded his head. "Spoke to a deputy about it just yesterday."

"Mind telling me what you told him?"

"Like I said, kids cross over the stream. The girl he showed me a picture of, well, I'd seen her. She and another girl about the same age. Caught them playing in the stream. They wandered about fifteen, twenty feet into my property. I caught sight of them when I was checking my snares."

"Did she seem okay?"

"She seemed fine and happy. The girls were picking flowers and laughing. They ran off as soon as I came up on them."

"When was that?"

"Couple days ago." Clem cocked an eye. "You sound more like a cop. I'm not in any trouble, am I?"

"Sorry. Old habits die hard."

"You used to be a cop?"

Hatch nodded. "In the Army." Every good cover story comes from a real place.

"My dad was in the Army too."

Hatch thought for a moment about the life she'd inherited in her father's passing. The road she walked because of it. And the road she was still on, the one same one that brought her here. All by honoring his code to help good people and hurt those responsible. Hatch had hurt many, but still felt no closer to peace. Maybe peace didn't come for some.

"Can you guess his job?" Clem fanned his arms toward the kitchen.

"Cook?"

"Not just any cook. The best damned cook in the Battle of France. Or at least the way he told it."

"Anyway, you didn't come here to listen to me prattle on." Clem squinted at the press badge on the counter. "Ask away, Miss Hatch, former Army police-turned-investigative-reporter."

"Hatch is fine."

"Okay then, Hatch. This is a small town, about as small as they get. All we got sometimes is talk, like my friend Harlin."

"And what is the gossip?"

"Well, we heard there was a problem with the child's deadbeat dad. Folks around here guess he didn't like his daughter being stuck with the white coats. Probably just took her, is all. I'm sure the deputies will have it sorted out soon enough."

"Let's hope."

"Sometimes that's all you can do."

Hatch put her fork to the shepherd's pie. "Sometimes you can do more."

HATCH FINISHED her meal and left twenty dollars as Clem's tip. She departed with a promise of returning for breakfast, then drove back to the motel.

As she pulled into the gravel lot, she saw Harlin's truck, along with another car, in the lot. A small dark blue four-door sedan in front of room number one. Hatch parked beside the truck and walked into the office.

Harlin peeked his head out. "Stopped by old Clem's?"

"As good as you said."

"Anything I can help you with?"

"Mind telling me who's in room number one?"

Harlin cocked an eyebrow. "Why don't you ask him yourself? He's right behind you."

Hatch turned to see a man in his mid-thirties with messy light brown hair. Tall with a thin build. A dark blue windbreaker flapped in the wind, exposing a plaid flannel as he walked across the parking lot. He looked more like a scarecrow than an actual man. His face glowed orange with each flick of the lighter cupped in his hands. He was working against the wind to light the cigarette in his mouth as Hatch made her way to the door.

"There's not going to be a problem, is there?" Harlin looked ready to defend Hatch's honor. "Don't need some type of lover's quarrel breakin' out in my lot."

"None of that. And there'll be no problems." She offered a quick smile. "At least, nothing that I can't handle," Hatch said under her breath as she pushed open the door and stepped back outside to meet the stranger.

The wind blew the smoke in Hatch's direction as he finally managed to light the cigarette. She walked up to the man who was now leaning against her Jeep.

"Can I help you?"

"My name is Ben Tracy."

Hatch saw the resemblance. Although Ben was younger, he looked more weathered than his brother. There was something in his eyes. He looked like he hadn't slept in days.

"Are you the one my brother sent?"

Hatch nodded. "That was you on the dirt road."

Nodding, he blew out a trail of smoke that danced around his face with the wind swirling. "I've been scoping that place out."

"I thought your brother told you to sit tight."

"Yeah, well, my brother and I haven't talked in a long time, so his ability to tell me what or what not to do doesn't hold the same weight."

"You look like you need some sleep."

"Sleep? How can I sleep when my daughter is missing? Everyone's looking at me."

"I'm here now. Let me see what I can do."

"Well, the police haven't done jack shit."

"I'm not the police. Nothing's going to get done tonight, I can tell you that. We'll start fresh in the morning. The best thing you can do for yourself right now is get some sleep. If we're going to figure out what happened to your daughter, I'm going to need your head clear. Fatigue is the breeding ground for mistakes."

"You sound just like him."

"We're cut from the same cloth."

"I hope you're as good as my brother says you are." He flicked the cigarette off into the distance.

"I'll see you in the morning."

He disappeared into his room. Hatch walked to hers two doors down. She looked back to see Harlin in the window. He gave a nod. Hatch returned it and went inside.

She pulled out her cell and called Jordan Tracy.

"How's it going?" Tracy answered on the second ring.

"Getting my footing. Stopped by the Eternal Light compound. No joy getting in tonight. Gonna try again in the morning."

"Your gut pulling you in any direction?"

"Too early to tell." She paused. "By the way, I met your brother."

"I told him to stay out of the way." Tracy spoke through gritted teeth. "Sometimes I wonder if he's got a brain inside that head of his."

"Would you stay out of the way? If your kid was missing?"

Tracy remained silent. "How's he doing?" He asked finally, the frustration replaced by concern.

"He's stretched thin."

"Do you think he's using again?"

"Not that I can see. It looked like he hadn't slept in days. We're going to reconnect in the morning once he's had a chance to rest. Then I'm going to take another run at the Eternal Light."

"Remember, we're off the books on this. You get a lead, you send it to the investigation agency. Let them run it down."

"I'll know more tomorrow."

"Watch your six."

"Always." Hatch ended the call.

She sat on the side of the bed and kicked her boots off. She didn't listen to the message Savage had left. Nor did she bother to reply to the text Cruise had sent. *Status?*

Unable to decide what to say to either man, Hatch opted for the next best option. Sleep.

THIRTEEN

SAVAGE SAT AT HIS DESK. THE CLOCK ON THE WALL SAID THE TIME WAS only nine-thirty, but the exhaustion that came at the end of a case like this left Savage drained. The fatigue in his body settled in like a weighted blanket, sinking him deeper into the swivel chair as he reviewed Sinclair's supplemental reports from the Graver case.

Sinclair had become a fine officer in the year plus, since Savage had taken over the small Hawk's Landing Sheriff's Office. He'd like to take credit for the growth and development of the young deputy, but aside from the guidance he provided, Savage knew much came from her interaction with Hatch when she'd acted as a de facto member of their department. Her confidence blossomed in the interim since Hatch's last departure and Sinclair had become his right hand.

Setting the report aside, he picked up a newspaper clipping. The dated pages of newsprint felt brittle in his fingers. He knew the words contained in the article forwards and backwards. He stared at it in his hands, just as he had a thousand times before since that day. "Hero Cop Stops Robbers." He hated every word.

Hero cop. He'd never felt that way about himself. He'd served with people he considered heroes and was honored to have been among them, but he never considered himself one. Hatch sat at the top of that list among a myriad of others. Others who the veteran sheriff had worked with during the years spent in Denver, both from his time on the street and his ten years of service in the department's Homicide unit.

The article described in detail the events leading up to the shooting death of a young man Savage shot, putting an end to a string of armed robberies. The article only made a passing mention that robbers were using Glock replica pellet guns to carry out their criminal enterprise.

Savage was first on scene and confronted the robbers. One of the young men turned his gun, which, in the split second he had to process the threat, he didn't realize was a fake. Savage, left without a choice, fired.

He'd seen photographs of the boy he'd shot countless times during the internal investigation and shooting review that followed. Savage was exonerated from any wrongdoing, but he still found it impossible to see the robber's face. Every time he recalled the events of that night, the face of the armed young man would never come into focus. It was as if his brain had created a filter, blurring the details.

In the years since the incident, Savage had learned, through research and speaking with others who'd been involved in a fatal officer involved shooting, that his brain had effectively buried the incident. A defense mechanism to the painful reality of taking another human being's life. Regardless of the circumstance, it left its mark.

In the stillness of his office, Savage wondered if Billy Graver could see the face of Glenn Miller. He wondered if killing the man who'd stolen his sister provided any peace or if it just added another horror to the boy's already fractured life.

The main line to the office rang. Barbara, the office's stalwart secretary, had gone home hours ago. Savage set the article aside and reached for the phone on his desk when he saw Sinclair had picked it up from her cubicle.

A moment later, the door to his office swung wide open. Becky Sinclair popped in. He slid the newspaper clipping under some files, hiding it.

"Yes, Becky?"

"Sheriff, a call for you on line one."

"Who is it?"

"FBI. It's a Dr. Sam Crenshaw with the FBI's forensics something-or-other."

"Okay, thanks, I've got it. And Becky, can you shut my door on your way out?" Sinclair shut the door. Savage picked up the phone on his desk and pressed line one.

"This is Sheriff Dalton Savage. How may I be of assistance this evening?"

"Hi. Sheriff Savage, this is Dr. Crenshaw with FBI forensics. Sorry for the late call."

Savage was surprised to hear a woman's voice. "No trouble at all. We're still wrapping up things on our end."

"As you know, the bureau has been assisting the state police forensic team in the lab. Since you're the originating agency, I wanted to keep you in the loop on a new development in the case."

"Go on."

"I thought you'd like to know, in the recovery and analysis of the remains found on the Miller property, we did locate in fact eighty-seven percent of the bone recovery for Amanda Graver, which is astounding considering the shallowness of the grave. Remains buried that long are rarely as complete."

"That's a good thing, right? Enough to determine cause of death?"

"Well, the chest cavity was relatively intact. For the most part. Her sternum had been shattered. Initial assessment would indicate the weapon was a blade. The entry would have been close to the heart. Death caused by the loss of blood." Crenshaw's delivery was robotic, as if she were reading the instructions of a refrigerator manual.

"Thank you for keeping me in the loop. I'll make the notations in our reports."

"There was something else." Crenshaw cleared her throat.

"What's that?"

"At the site, and during the recovery of Amanda Miller's bones, we found another set."

"You mean another victim?"

"Yes. Though, this one is not as complete."

Savage let out a long, slow exhale. "Another child?"

"Afraid so." Some of the stiffness left Crenshaw's voice. "The body returns to a missing persons case out of Wilson County, Tennessee. Going back fifteen years."

"Fifteen years." Savage repeated the words. A lot of time and miles between those two sets of bones.

"The state police have already notified the sheriff's office down there. I can give you the contact information for the investigator working the case should you need to conduct any follow up."

She gave Savage the information, and the call ended. Savage stared at the detective's information he'd just jotted down. Looking at his phone, there was no call back from Hatch. He dialed the number Crenshaw had given him.

Savage planned on leaving a message and was surprised when his call was answered.

"Hello?" The voice on the other end sounded meek.

"This is Dalton Savage, the Sheriff up in Hawk's Landing, Colorado. I'm trying to reach a Detective Thorpe with the Wilson County Sheriff's."

"Speaking." Thorpe spoke up, but only by a little. "I guess you got the call about the bones."

"I did. Anything you can tell me about the case?"

"I can tell you it's been a long time in the coming since I've had a lead. I'm working to piece the connection together but having a bit of trouble."

"If I can help in any way, I will."

"I'm working solo on this and could sure use it."

Savage looked at one of the photographs from the dig site where the bones had been discovered and began thinking of the other family, whose wounds had remained opened for nearly two decades. "Look for me tomorrow."

"Not sure that's necessary."

"I like to see things through. Especially, when it's a case involving children."

"I'm not going to lie, the extra hand might be a nice change of pace."

Savage ended the call with Thorpe. He then went online and purchased the first flight out of Denver for the following morning.

Returning the clipping to the bottom recesses of his desk, Savage closed the drawer and stood. He left his office and walked over to Sinclair who was typing the notes from their meeting with Graver earlier.

Sinclair looked up at him as Savage stopped next to the cubicle wall. "So what'd the feds want?"

"They found another set of bones at Amanda's gravesite."

Sinclair's mouth dropped wide as she fumbled for words. "Who?"

"A girl who disappeared out of Tennessee about fifteen years ago," Savage said.

"Glenn Miller was a serial?" The shock subsided a bit.

"That's what I'm going to try to figure out. I'm going to be heading there tomorrow morning to put my eyes on this thing." Savage looked around the empty office space. "You're going to be in charge while I'm gone."

"Me?"

"I can't think of anybody better." Savage smiled.

"That's because there isn't anybody else. Besides Littleton."

"True." Littleton was still as green as they come. Sinclair had moved light years ahead of her patrol counterpart. "But regardless, if there was, I would still choose you."

Sinclair's cheeks reddened. It reminded Savage of the way Hatch turned bright red at the first sign of any emotional discomfort. "Listen, Becky, I know it seems like a lot, but you're ready. You can keep this place running like a well-oiled machine. I'm confident you can handle anything that comes your way."

"At least that makes one of us," Sinclair muttered.

"I've been around the block a time or two. And I can speak from experience, how you handled yourself on the Miller scene proved beyond a shadow of doubt that you're ready, whether you realize it or not."

"Thanks."

"I'll be back in a day or so."

Denver was about six hours away. He'd have to pack fast if he planned on making the early morning flight. Jumping in his SUV, he raced off into the night, hoping tomorrow would bring some closure to both the case and the victim's family.

FOURTEEN

HATCH ROSE JUST BEFORE DAWN. SHE'D GONE ON A QUICK THREE-MILER to the main road, doubling back before seeing more than a couple of trailer homes sparsely lining the way into town. She wanted to get an early start to the day and return to the Eternal Light compound.

Showered and dressed, Hatch stopped by the main office, grabbed two cups of coffee, and headed for the door.

"Get your story yet?" Harlin called from the back, rolling himself into view on his office chair.

"Not yet."

"Everything okay with our friend in room one?"

"Yeah, he's good. Nothing to worry about there."

"Okay." Harlin didn't look convinced. "Like I told you last night—those Tunics open their doors at sunrise. Keep 'em open 'til it sets."

"I thought you said they keep to themselves."

"They open the gates so that anybody can find their way in. Some-thin' to do with the door to salvation needing the light of day."

"What happens if someone needs salvation after dark?"

"Guess they're shit out of luck."

Hatch left the office and went over to Ben's room. Both hands occupied by the coffee, Hatch gave three taps of her boot to the door's metal kick plate. The door opened and Ben looked better than last night. The dark circles under his eyes were less pronounced.

"Looks like you got some rest." Hatch offered him a cup with a couple packs of sugar and a non-dairy creamer on top of the lid. "Didn't know how you take it."

"Black is just fine." Ben took the coffee. Setting the cream and sugar on the television, he grabbed his jacket.

"I'd like to pick your brain over breakfast before I begin."

"Fair enough." He picked up a set of keys off a small table near the door.

"I'll drive." Hatch walked over to the Jeep and climbed inside. Ben joined her and they headed into town.

Less than ten minutes later, they were seated at Clem's. She'd opted for a booth tucked in the back. Sitting with her back against the wall, she looked past Ben to the patrons enjoying their breakfast, accompanied by a side of gossip.

"We're the talk of the town," Hatch said.

Clem came out from the kitchen. His thin white mustache curled up in a smile at the sight of Hatch. A smile that disappeared the moment he saw her companion. The restaurant owner-chef-waiter approached.

"Looks like you brought company." Clem approached with a coffee pot in hand.

"Clem, meet Ben Tracy. He's the father of the little girl who went missing."

Clem cast a questioning eye over Ben. "I've seen you in here over the last couple days." Clem turned and shot an eye back towards the other customers looking over at Hatch's companion, whispering amongst themselves.

"Whatever they're saying about Ben's involvement, they got it all wrong." Hatch said.

"One of your sources?" Clem asked.

"The best kind. The horse's mouth."

Clem turned to Ben. "I'm real sorry to hear about your little girl. The whole town's shook up about it. And never mind those whispers, just gives them something to do. Y'all look like you could use a good meal."

"Whatever your breakfast special is, as long as it comes with a bit of that cornbread." Hatch said.

"Just took it out of the pan before coming over here. And you?" Clem asked Ben.

"I'll have what she's having."

Clem filled both their mugs with coffee and returned to the kitchen.

"That's the friendliest reception I've gotten since coming into town." Ben said.

"That's how it goes in small towns like this. I grew up in one." Hatch said.

"Me too. Not this small, though."

"Is that where you met Kyla's mom?"

"No. Years later, I was a long-haul trucker. It was a good gig and I liked it. Having a brother like Jordan who went off and served his country, I wanted to cut my own path. Didn't want to follow his footsteps or live in his shadow. After high school, I set out on my own. I've always been a bit of a drifter."

"Me too," Hatch said.

"Kind of fell in love with the trucking gig. Loved being on the open road and loved seeing the country that people take for granted when they fly over. I like the energy of a rest stop and the conversations with people you meet along the way. I met Dot—short for Dorothy, even had a little Scottie named Toto just for kicks—at one of those truck stops after a long stretch. She was a waitress. And we just clicked. I took routes that enabled me to stop through as often as I could. Everything happened fast after that. Kyla was an uh-oh, but not in a bad way. I was head over heels for Dot and always planned to marry her, but I guess it wasn't in the cards."

"If you don't mind me asking, what happened between the two of you?"

"The same road that brought us together tore us apart. We moved into a small place outside of Augusta, Georgia. A drunk driver sent me into a guard rail, messed my back up pretty good. Docs put me on some pain meds. I guess it started there. The pain meds led me to other things, and before I knew it, I was shooting up between my toes to hide it from Dot. But she came from a hard life and a broken home, so it wasn't long before she started seeing the signs. But I lied, like all addicts lie. Then I got into another crash. This time there was no other driver to blame, just me. I T-boned a small four door when I blew a red at an intersection and took the life of a businessman on his way home from a conference. I took a DUI manslaughter charge. No choice after they took blood tox from me after the crash. There was no more lying to Dot at that point. It was there in black and white in the police report, the heroin in my system at the time. Kyla was seven. I got an eight-year sentence reduced to four for good behavior."

"And how come it took you until now to try to contact your daughter?"

"Even though I was out on good behavior, I hadn't behaved well inside of prison. Do you know it's just about as easy to get drugs inside as it was outside?"

"I do. I spent time as a military police officer. Prisons are prisons. Even in the military ones, drugs found their way inside."

"When I came out I was just as strung out, maybe more so than when I'd gone in. I tracked Dot and Kyla down, but I was high when I found Dot working as a waitress again. She saw the addiction in my eyes and the freshness of the track marks on my arms." Rolling his sleeve up, he slightly exposed the depressions in his skin. "I wear long sleeves now, even in the heat of the summer."

Hatch reached for her coffee. The sleeve of her lightweight sweat-shirt slid up, exposing more of her right arm. "Everybody has scars, some are just easier to see. My father used to say, 'Until you walk a mile in someone's shoes...'"

Ben nodded his head and took a sip of his coffee. "I don't think anyone would want mine. I wore out a lot of welcomes and burned a lot of bridges in my life. With my family, my friends—but the most devastating to me is my daughter. And when Dot had seen me that way, she took Kyla and ran. Then I disappeared into a drug-induced haze that nearly left me dead, but at the end of it, I found help."

Ben reached into his pocket and pulled out a coin. "One year sober. I said I would get this coin in my hand before I tried to make peace with Dot and reestablish my relationship with Kyla, but they were harder to find, and it took me a while of searching."

"How'd you find them here?"

"She had distant family outside of Nashville in Mt. Juliet. I asked about her over there and they said, last they had heard, she was working as a clerk at the grocery in Jericho Falls. By the time I got here, she'd taken up with that commune. That's pretty much it. I tried to speak to Dot, but The Shepherd and his guard dog, the big mute, wouldn't let me. I planned to begin the legal battle and even retained an attorney. Everyone told me I've got an uphill battle. The Eternal Light doesn't recognize our court system, so serving them and getting any action takes a lot of work on the court's behalf, and it's going to take a lot to prove I'm even worthy of the fight after all these years."

Hatch looked at the man across from her and smiled. "I think you're worth the fight."

Just then, Clem returned with the two breakfast specials carried on one arm and a plate with two big pieces of cornbread on the other.

"Make sure you eat while you can. If these storms start hitting and the power goes out, won't be much in the way of food."

Clem left them to enjoy their meal.

———

HATCH DABBED her fingertip onto the plate, extracting the last of the crumbs. The sweet taste of Clem's homemade cornbread lingered in her mouth as she left the restaurant. The breeze cleared a path through the muggy mid-morning air. A girl dressed in a white gown danced around the flagpole outside of the diner.

The child's hair, the color of sunlight, was done in braids, the ends of which bounced loosely as she was lost in her dance. She carried a small wicker basket of freshly picked flowers.

A man wearing a long tunic was talking to the hardware shop owner next door to Clem's. She overheard a bit of the conversation. A trade for nails and screws was being hashed out between the two men, but Hatch wasn't as interested in the barter as much as she was the little girl.

Aside from her hair color, everything else about the child was nearly identical to the photo Hatch had of Kyla. The pang of sadness rippling through Ben as he caught sight of the carefree girl was obvious.

Hatch gave a small wave of her hand. The girl stopped. She eyed Hatch for a moment. Caution giving way, the girl smiled. Hatch approached, ignoring Ben's hushed advice not to bother.

"Hi." Hatch hunched low, meeting the child's eyes, a dazzling blue, much like the deep cobalt of Cruise. "I'm Hatch."

"That's a funny name." The girl giggled. "I'm Marigold."

Hatch thought of Daphne. Her Daffodil. The same sense of wonderment danced in the bright eyes staring back at Hatch.

"I'm looking for a little girl. About your age." Hatch pulled out her cellphone and swiped to a picture of Kyla. She held it out for Marigold to see.

The little girl turned her head. She brought up the hand holding the basket of flowers, further shielding herself from the image on the screen. Marigold looked like Dracula fending off the cross.

"Do not speak to her!" The voice came from the man in the white tunic who had left his bartering and was fast approaching.

Hatch put her hands up. "I was just asking your daughter about a little girl we're looking for. I didn't mean to offend anyone."

The girl's father positioned himself between Marigold and Hatch.

"I just wanted to show her a picture." Hatch gestured to the phone in her hand.

"She is forbidden to look at such devices. They provide access to the devil's tongue."

"Maybe you can speak to me, then?"

"If you want answers, then you must seek The Shepherd." He offered nothing else before turning his back to Hatch. The father took his daughter by the hand and walked away toward a horse-drawn buggy. Marigold looked back at Hatch just before climbing into the carriage. The smile from earlier was gone completely.

"That went well," Ben said.

"I'm only getting started." Hatch walked toward the Jeep as the carriage pulled away. "I guess we know who we have to talk to next. And I'd like to get there before our new friend does."

FIFTEEN

SAVAGE TOOK THE EARLY MORNING DIRECT FLIGHT FROM DENVER TO Nashville, arriving just before noon. He tried to use the flight time to catch up on the sleep stolen by the all-night drive to the airport, but he only managed disjointed and fitful naps. Upon reaching the rental car agency, Savage had learned that all the SUVs had been rented, with the last one taken the day before. He was left with two choices: A light green Dodge Neon, or a white Caprice. He had opted for the Chevy.

Savage took I-40 East toward Lebanon, where the Wilson County Sheriff's Office was located. Traffic was light, and he made good time, but just outside of Lebanon, a tree branch had fallen on a car and traffic was at a standstill, adding an extra hour to his trip. It was midday by the time Savage arrived.

A large rectangular concrete building housed both the sheriff's office and the Wilson County jail. The main entrance offered visitor access to both facilities. Savage parked in the visitor lot in front and went inside. Although separated by thick concrete walls, the murmured echoes from within the jail resonated in the lobby space.

A heavyset woman in a floral dress sat on a bench crying and dabbing her tears with a handkerchief. She was surrounded by several children, some consoling their grieving mother, others taking her distracted state as an opportunity to turn the lobby into a jungle gym.

Savage bypassed the chaos and walked to the main desk. He pressed the button to talk. There was a civilian seated on the other side of the thick bullet-resistant glass. Savage pressed his badge and ID against the fingerprint-smeared barrier.

"Sheriff Dalton Savage, here to see Detective James Thorpe. I'm a little later than I planned, but he's expecting me."

"Just a moment, sugar," the receptionist said.

She pushed herself back on a rolling chair and picked up a phone, cradling it between her head and neck. Punching in a four-digit number, she had a brief conversation that Savage couldn't hear through the divider in front of him or the crying behind him.

She rolled back his way. "He'll be with you in a moment. Have a seat if you can find one."

Savage eyed the lobby. Deciding not to invade the personal space of the grieving woman, he stood off to the side, reached into his pocket, and popped a couple of pieces of black licorice into his mouth.

A door marked, "Law Enforcement Access Only," to the left of the main desk opened. Standing in the doorway was a man of average height. He had a short haircut, a hair longer than a military high-and-tight, and a thick mustache neatly groomed curled over his upper lip, stopping at the corners of his mouth. He wore a lightweight gray sweater vest over a button-up shirt and tie. Savage noticed the clean lines pressed along the edges of his shirt and slacks. He was so thin that even the sweater vest barely gave form to his chest.

"Sheriff Savage?"

"Dalton is fine."

"Jim Thorpe." The detective extended a hand, and they shook.

"Thanks for meeting with me." Dalton said

"Thanks for flying all the way here. Like I told you on the phone, I'm not sure it's worth your effort though." Thorpe said.

"This was one of those cases that I wanted to see all the way through, you know what I mean?"

Thorpe nodded.

"I'd like to see what you have on the investigation and see where we can connect the dots, because right now, I'm drawing blanks."

"Follow me down the rabbit hole." Thorpe led Savage inside. "I'm not sure the size of the sheriff's office you're coming from, but we run about two hundred and sixty-five here, thirty in the Bureau."

"Well, you've got about ten times the number in your Bureau than I have in my whole agency, but I spent the majority of my career in Denver. Ten years in homicide."

Thorpe gave a nod of his head. "I bet you've seen some things."

"I've worn both hats, and I can say that evil exists in both the big city and the small town."

"Ain't that the truth." Thorpe led Savage down a hallway. "The first floor and down houses our patrol guys. Second floor is our Bureau admins."

Thorpe bypassed the elevator and made his way to a side stairwell. A sign said, "Prisoner Intake and Holding."

"We're not going to your office?"

"We are. Well, an office of sorts. This case is kind of my baby. I've been working it for over ten years. It became a bit overwhelming, and after reaching a peace accord with my lieutenant, they gave me a separate space away from the other detectives."

Thorpe ran his ID badge over a security panel. The door buzzed loudly and Thorpe pulled it open. The noise from the jail echoed through the stairwell. As Thorpe headed down, two detectives with long hair and beards and wearing street clothes passed them coming up.

"Hey Thorpenado. Taking a friend to the cave?" The other detective laughed, neither slowing to wait for Thorpe's response.

"Narc guys. They get a lot done, but they can be assholes." Thorpe said.

"That's true of big cities and small towns. Everybody's got one." Savage said.

They went down one flight of stairs and entered the main holding area. They walked between four sets of holding cells. The ten-by-twenty iron-barred spaces were separated by concrete walls, two on each side.

Savage heard the cacophony of noise. Men crying for their phone call, others pleading their innocence, some threatening violence. Savage had heard it all before.

Both men passed by without tossing a glance at the men in the cages, avoiding engaging them in any way, none of which would have been fruitful.

The noise faded as they turned a corner and moved along a hallway. Narrower, this one was lined with offices for intake processing, administrative efforts, and moving the masses through the penal system. Thorpe took Savage to a door at the end of the hall. There was a piece of paper stuck to the door that said, "The Cave."

"I used to tear them down. Now, I just don't care."

This door didn't have an electric lock like the others. It required a key, which Thorpe produced from the key chain in his pocket, connected to his belt with a lanyard. He unlocked both the deadbolt and the knob's lock.

"Enter at your own risk. It's a work in progress." Thorpe said.

"I'm sure I can handle it." Savage replied.

As they entered, a light on a sensor activated, bathing the small ten-by-ten room in its pale glow. Almost every single inch of the room's four walls was covered with everything from crime scene photos to newspaper articles, to bits and pieces of police reports.

Behind a cluttered desk on the far wall was a large map of Tennessee. Overlapping concentric circles marked in red pen covered the map, moving along in a snakelike pattern that nearly split the map in two.

"What's the meaning of the circles?"

"Where the girls went missing. The X's mark where they were last seen. The circle marks the areas searched."

"Tell me more about the girl we found, or at least the parts that we found in Colorado."

"Erika Beaumont, she went missing about ten years ago. She was eleven years old at the time."

"And there was no trace?"

"It was a tough one. The report was delayed. It followed a bad tornado. There was a lot of damage from that one. We were flooded with a ton of missing person cases. That always happens after a big one, but as recovery efforts proceeded and either the dead or the living were found, one remained missing. Erika Beaumont. But now we have her remains, or at least enough to get a positive ID. From what you've told me, it sounds like your Glen Miller might've been a serial."

"It looks that way," Savage said. "I'm surprised the FBI hasn't jumped on this yet."

"They may come around. I forwarded it to them, but this won't be the first time. One of the reasons I've been relegated to the basement here, when this story broke of the girl missing after the tornado, the newspaper had labeled him the Twister Man. The FBI was interested, but when leads dried up and I was left with nothing but conjecture and no substance to back it, the FBI pulled back. My sheriff wasn't real keen and Twister Man became somewhat of an inside joke around the department."

"Glen Miller's background is pretty hazy. We don't know much about him, just that he came to Hawks Landing about ten years ago."

"It matches the timeline. Maybe he killed Erika and got spooked. Maybe she was his first. I know serials, they like to keep a token."

"You work many before?"

Thorpe shook his head. "No, but I read a lot."

"I worked two in Denver. They're tough puzzles, but you're right about the token thing. They usually leave things behind, either because they want to get caught or they want to stay connected to the victim, or they want notoriety. There's a thousand reasons for why serials act the way they do. "

"For my sheriff, it's a closed case." Thorpe said.

"But you don't see it that way." Savage replied.

"All those circles, all those missing girls, all between the ages of ten and twelve years old, and all following a major tornado."

"Have there been any since Beaumont disappeared?"

"Two—actually, three. One girl had reportedly escaped."

"Was she able to identify him, give any specifics?"

"Well, she'd just turned ten." Thorpe walked over to a drawing. "McKenzie Blackmore, she drew this."

Savage stepped closer to examine the picture. It looked like a stick figure with arms like tree branches. Swirls of black crayon formed a recognizable tornado and set inside it were dark black eyes.

"I ran a full forensic interview. This is the drawing she made for me, and the one she swore tried to take her. I know what it looks like, but when I talked to the girl, she was onto something."

"Let me guess." Savage looked around the confines of the room. "Your bosses didn't see it that way."

"Nope. Thus, Thorpenado was born. The man responsible for hunting the Twister Man, a boogie man, but one I knew existed. Too bad another child had to die before we could put a face to the monster."

"At least it's over now." Savage scanned the ten-plus years of investigative efforts strewn across the Thorpe's cave. His eyes settled on McKenzie Blackmore's depiction of her attacker; the monster Billy Graver had put to rest. The killer's death left Savage with more questions than answers.

SIXTEEN

HATCH PASSED THE CARRIAGE BACK IN TOWN AND WAS NOW MILES ahead, having already passed Clem's red mailbox. She turned onto the dirt road to the Eternal Light compound. Ben sat in the passenger seat, twirling a cigarette between his middle and forefinger.

"I'm going to park at the bend where you were posted last night." Hatch slowed to a stop. "I want you to wait here."

" Are you kidding?"

"If I'm going to have any chance of meeting with the preacher, it's going to be without you at my side." Hatch could see from the distraught father's pained expression that this was not sitting well. "It'd look a bit off if I walk in with the father of the missing girl. It'll be a lot harder to sell my backstory."

"I get it."

Hatch grabbed her notepad that was tucked between her seat and the center console before exiting the Jeep. She held the door open for a moment. "Remember when you asked me what my specialty was?"

Ben stopped the cigarette in mid twirl and nodded.

"Interview and interrogation." Hatch closed the door and followed the dirt path around the bend.

The wooden gates to the compound were open wide. A light

drizzle fell, settling the dusty road. She heard a voice rise over the gentle rustle of leaves in the late morning breeze. Beyond the gates was a circle of people, like the night before, except there was no fire roaring and no singing.

Instead, one man stood at the center in front of a large stone altar, commanding the full attention of all present. The others sat cross-legged on the ground and held their hands up in worship. They swayed like branches in the wind, entranced by the sermon or the man delivering it, or both.

Hatch came to the gate and saw no sign of the shadowed giant who blocked her access the previous night. She stood at the threshold of the entrance and listened.

"When Eve was led astray in the Garden, her innocence was unprepared for the devil's forked tongue. And with the hissed words whispered in her ear, Eden was shattered. We will not be led astray. We see the innocence of our young, the eyes with which they behold the world, the purity of their hearts and souls. It is our duty to take refuge and shelter from the evils of this world, to protect our young before that age of transcendence, that moment when child and woman meet at the turning. We don't turn our eyes from it. Instead, we look upon that change, and we ready the child for the world that awaits, a world we keep at bay. How long have our walls stood while those outside of them are ravaged by the forces of nature commanded by God's heralding angels? When the water rises after heavy rains, and the river that runs through floods our banks, what do we do?"

"Rejoice," the group chanted in unison.

"Rejoice and celebrate." The Shepherd smiled and nodded, taking the time to make eye contact with each of his followers, even the young children who sat attentively by their mothers' sides. "What the world has stolen from you, I cannot give back, but I can assure you that the harms of the outside world will not touch you again, for I am The Shepherd. "

"And we are your flock," again the chant in unison.

"In the fold you shall stay, my care I shall provide. The gift of Eden has been reclaimed. Those who seek it will find us, as they always do.

Like Noah before the flood, we shall stand against the rising tides and avoid the temptations of man. When furious winds blow and uproot trees, what do we do?"

"Rejoice."

"That's right. When the wolf is at our gates, I will be your Shepherd."

"And we will be your flock."

The preacher shot a gaze at Hatch. A thick rope loosely wrapped around the preacher's midline kept his tunic down. He held out his left hand, moving it back and forth in the air, the congregation bowing their heads as it passed by overhead. The long wooden staff in his right hand remained firmly planted at his side. The scene reminded Hatch of her religious education classes and the picture of Moses parting the Red Sea.

"There is plenty of work to be done in preparation for tomorrow's Rise." The preacher locked eyes with Hatch. "We fear not the approaching darkness, because I am the light!"

"Light eternal." The crowd lifted their voices skyward.

The circle dissolved into a whirl of white. Standing at its center was The Shepherd.

The sermon ended, and the followers began collecting themselves, returning to whatever chores lay waiting. Hatch waited until The Shepherd finished speaking with the congregants who lingered. She watched as he met each person with a kind hand and warm smile.

As the last cleared, Hatch locked eyes with the preacher. She offered a friendly wave of her hand and held up her badge while standing at the entrance.

The Shepherd leveled his gaze at Hatch. The smile he'd shared with the other worshipers was gone. He planted the long staff in the earth before him and began making his way to her. Hatch noticed that the walking stick was not just a showpiece. The Shepherd favored his right side and walked with a slight limp he worked hard at hiding.

SEVENTEEN

THE SHEPHERD MADE HIS WAY OVER TO HATCH. AS HE DREW CLOSER, HIS mouth turned up in a friendly smile, one that to Hatch appeared to be more forced than when he'd delivered his sermon. He was younger, or at least younger looking than she'd expected. Hatch guessed at late thirties or early forties. It was hard to tell. Although draped in a similar tunic worn by the others, Hatch noticed his trim build and athletic shoulders. His jet-black hair was long, with ends that curled before touching his shoulders.

Hatch stood her ground and played the part of the eager, but polite, reporter. "I'm Rachel Hatch, with The Blaze. I stopped by last night but was turned away. I left a card with someone, but—"

"Yes...I heard." The preacher stopped a few feet from Hatch, his smile never leaving his face. His eyes burned with intensity. "Mathias is our gatekeeper. No visitors are allowed after dark."

"I didn't know." Hatch feigned ignorance.

"No matter. How were you to know?" The smile dropped. "I hope you didn't misinterpret his note as a means of disrespect. Long ago Mathias took a vow of silence."

"Is that a requirement within your community?"

"Oh, no. Silence is not for everyone. For some, it proves too much.

Not for our Mathias. He has shouldered its burden for a very long time."

"How long is long?" Hatch asked as she adjusted the notepad in her hand.

"Fifteen years, give or take."

"Fifteen years is a long time to hold one's tongue." Hatch thought of the fifteen years she'd spent away from her home and the path she was on now that continued to delay her return.

The Shepherd fanned a hand out in a wide sweeping motion toward the scattering crowd of followers dressed in white. "Everybody chooses their path. For some, silence is a way to turn a better ear to God's word."

Hatch counted a total of twenty-eight who'd gathered for the morning's sermon. She scanned for Kyla's mother, using a dated picture shown to her by Ben. Hatch caught a glimpse of her disappearing behind a wood house. She wondered if a mother who'd just lost her child would remain silent.

"How can I help you this morning?" The Shepherd asked.

"I'm doing a piece on your community." Hatch said.

"Why?"

"My editor assigned it to me yesterday. I go where the story takes me." Hatch held back, in asking about Kyla. Effective interview and interrogation always started with rapport building. Trust, even if the basis of its formation is built around a ruse like Hatch's cover, was the foundation of every successful intel gathering session.

"And what do you hope to accomplish in this journalistic pursuit?"

"The truth." Hatch caught a slight narrowing in The Shepherd's eyes. "A lot of people say the Eternal Light is another Branch Davidian in the making."

"The judgments cast by those outside these walls hold no relevance. My goal is to spread the Word. I believe nothing happens by chance. Maybe your article will shine a light and become a beacon calling any lost souls home."

"Then you'll be willing to speak with me?"

"Of course. As long as you take no photographs or videos."

Hatch had hoped to photograph as many of the Eternal Light followers as she could and send the images to Jordan Tracy to run against facial recognition software. She wanted to compile as much as possible about the people within the confines of these walls. "Are you sure I couldn't snap a couple of photos? Readers love a good picture. Helps sell these days."

"I'm afraid it's out of the question. You're going to have to paint any pictures with your words."

"Fair enough." Hatch fumbled with her cellphone as she exchanged it for the notepad and pen in her satchel, snapping a photo of the preacher as she dropped the phone into the bag. "Let's start with why you call yourself The Shepherd."

"Because that is what I am."

Hatch jotted a note in the pad.

"What's your name? I'd like to note your true name for my article."

"That is my true name. No other one exists now. The me of before is not connected with the me of now, although tendrils of the past always linger."

The Shepherd led Hatch inside. The other followers were moving about, carrying on their daily tasks. A woman nearby, whose tunic was held by a sash rather than a rope, worked the handle of a butter churn while the three-year-old at her side held the wooden rod.

"Everybody does their part here, even the children."

"To what end?" Hatch asked.

"Enlightenment. Here, we tune out the outside world. We listen to the call of nature. We believe that the word of God can be found there if one is willing to listen. I try to provide a place for that connection, unimpeded."

"How many people live here?"

"There are twenty-eight among us now, myself included."

Hatch wondered if Kyla was listed in that twenty-eight or if he had already deleted her from the roster. "How do you recruit?"

The Shepherd laughed to himself. "I don't 'recruit,' as you put it. The Lord does all the recruiting I need, calling to people in different ways. The lives these people lived before they came to me, and the reasons why, all differ. Some seek refuge from a world that treated them harshly. Others sought divinity."

"Tell me a little bit about the Eternal Light. It's based in Christianity, correct?"

"Every house needs a foundation. When I first took to this calling, I took a vow of silence myself. Unlike my friend Mathias there, after a year I broke mine at God's command so that I may share the word that I discovered in my silence, a year without speaking."

Hatch scribbled into her pad, playing the part of the reporter to a fault. "That must've been tough," Hatch said, looking up.

"It comes with its challenge, yes, but it opened my ears and eyes to things that I had missed. During that time, I went line by line through the King James Bible, rewriting it in my own hand, word by word. I found myself transfixed by the deeper meaning, by the words that weren't written. I heard it in the screech of the hawks above. I saw it in the winds and rains, floods and famines, and I added those things that were missing, the parts that weren't whole for me, the parts that I heard whispered in my ears."

"So, you hear God speak to you?" Hatch put a notation with a question mark.

"Yes, I do. Is that so strange to believe?"

Hatch thought of her father, and his voice that had come back to her on more than one occasion, typically in a time of need. There were times when she could feel him standing there with her as she faced the darkness.

"I guess not," Hatch said.

"Being human, we naturally see things through our own skewed perspective."

"And you're not?"

"I guess it could be seen by some that my interpretation is a perversion of scripture. I see it more as a rewriting. In the thousands of years since the writing of the Bible, much has been changed, much has been interpreted. Divisions and wars have been fought, and more lives lost and blood spilled in the name of God than any other cause in history, and we just continue to rage. His ideologies are challenged.

But I am just one voice. Hopefully, someday it'll be heard above the noise."

"Were you raised in a religious household?"

"Not in comparison to what I am doing now, and not any stricter than most, church on Sundays, Bible school as a kid. I doubt my family even goes anymore."

"Do you have any contact with them?"

"The rules of my community would be nothing if I didn't follow them myself."

"How long has it been since you had contact with them?"

"Since we came here."

"How long have you been here in Jericho Falls?"

"Going on fifteen years now."

"Why here?"

"Why not? But it was my Shepherd that led me here. Others followed or joined along the way."

Hatch cocked an eyebrow. "And where is he now?"

"He is no longer with us."

"So he left?"

"We parted ways and he passed his staff to me."

"Where is he now?"

"Your guess is as good as mine. Once a member leaves the community, there is no other contact unless they return."

Hatch looked at the walking staff in The Shepherd's hand. There were misshapen figure eights of varying sizes burned into the wood throughout, covering the stick from top to bottom. "Does the eight hold significance to your belief structure?"

"Not an eight, Miss Hatch. It's the infinity symbol, because we see God in everything, most importantly at the point of transcendence."

Hatch looked around at the houses, counting ten in two neat columns of five, with several fire pits staged at the center of the divide between the two rows.

"How much of the land beyond the commune is yours?"

"Three hundred acres belong to the Eternal Light." The Shepherd scanned his flock and the woodland area beyond.

"That must've cost a pretty penny."

"My previous life, which I don't wish to talk about, provided many things in the way of resources. It is to that end that I was able to secure the land. Since it was bought outright, we have no dealings with taxes since there is no profit within these walls."

"How do you ensure the safety of your people?"

"The gate that kept you out last night holds strong. Built from fallen timbers, it has served us these many years." He gestured toward the opening. "And God willing, for many more to come."

"Beyond barring outsiders, how do you provide protection within its walls? How do you know that the people who come here are not criminals?"

"Simple. The Lord has bestowed me with the ability to see into the heart of man."

Hatch's understanding of how to read people was grounded in the kinesthetic science, supporting the interpretation of body language as a measure for which to read deception. Listening to The Shepherd and analyzing the micro gestures as he spoke, Hatch had drawn two conclusions. Either the leader of the Eternal Way truly believed the things he was saying, or he was an incredible liar. For Hatch, it was too early to tell which.

"So no background checks or inquiries into new members?" Hatch asked.

"Our ears are always open to listen should someone feel compelled to discuss their life beyond the walls. But to answer your question more directly. No, we do not check."

"Then in theory, anybody, regardless of their past, could move undetected among your people."

"Anything is possible." There was a dismissiveness in his tone. "But that is why I'm here. When one does not embrace our way of life, they are simply asked to leave. When they come, their slate is wiped clean. When they leave, the responsibility for how they carry forward with that clean slate is upon their shoulders."

"So, a criminal could come in here, no questions asked, and join your flock?"

"Potentially. Sure. But if you remember the Bible, Saul, who later became known as Paul and is often referred to as the thirteenth apostle, was responsible for the murder of the Apostle Stephen. He heard God's word call out to him in his darkest hour. He became a voice of Christianity. So, we here at the Eternal Light do not judge anyone by past indiscretions. Those who walk through that gate and join my flock are judged by the actions they take while they are with us, not by their past, no matter how good or how bad one might be."

"And can those who come here choose to leave?"

A smile spread across The Shepherd's face. "You think they're held against their will? Free will was a gift given to man. It's the same gift that I give each and every one of my flock. Should they desire to leave, they are free to do so. Over the years, some have. Our ranks diminish and then they're replenished."

"What about medical care and schooling?"

"We have all of that. Our schooling is somewhat different from what you may have experienced, but the fundamentals of interacting with the world around us are intact. We teach community. We teach how to love and cherish each other. Regardless of anyone's prior life experience, they are all taught the trade of the Son. And we use that skill when life demands, both for us and for those beyond our walls."

"Like when you helped to rebuild the town last year?"

"We do what we can."

"In the hopes of bringing more people into your flock?"

"It would be nice if it worked that way, but often it doesn't. Though a few townsfolk have seen the goodness in what we do and have joined our ranks."

"Would I be able to speak to some of your followers?"

"No."

Hatch stopped scribbling notes into the pad and looked up.

"I have made a promise to them from the moment they entered to protect them. I must act as an intermediary and stand between the devil's whispers and their delicate ears."

Just as Hatch was about to press further in the hopes of speaking with Dot, the clop of a horse's hooves from the trail behind her drew her attention. She turned to see the man from the hardware store with the young Marigold sitting alongside.

"How did it go in town?" The Shepherd asked as the carriage drew to a stop nearby. The man dismounted and cast a glare at Hatch as he walked past her and whispered something in The Shepherd's ear, who only nodded in return. "It seems you've already attempted to speak to one of my followers. The child, for that matter. And it appears, Miss Hatch, that there is more to the story you're digging at."

"I'm just trying to get the full picture of what happened. A little girl went missing. I think that warrants as much attention as possible."

"You should've led with that."

"Would you have permitted me to enter, had I?"

"Probably not."

Marigold hopped down from the carriage and skipped her way over to her father's side. She played with a braid with one hand, still holding the basket of flowers with the other.

"I think it's time you leave, Miss Hatch. You may not find my gates open to you when you return."

Hatch opened her mouth to speak but the child spoke first. In a sweet, lyrical voice, she looked up at The Shepherd. "Shepherd, let her see my Rise. Let her understand the beauty of transcendence. Maybe she's just forgotten."

"You ask a lot, my little Marigold." Turning his gaze to Hatch. "We do not question the innocence of a child here. In fact, the opposite is true. Their wisdom comes in a purity we no longer connect to. If by her request, she'd like you to attend her ceremony tomorrow, I'm obliged to make the offer. It is your choice to accept or decline."

Hatch looked at the little girl. "I'll be here," she said.

Marigold stepped closer to Hatch, her father's arm catching her by the shoulder, halting her. The girl then reached into her basket and extended a flower toward Hatch, who took it and smiled.

"It begins at sunrise when God's first light touches the altar," her voice a whisper just above the breeze.

Then, a tall man walked toward them from behind a cluster of trees in the wood line, just beyond the closest house.

"Mathias," The Shepherd said. "Please see our visitor out."

His white tunic was dirt-covered and showed the toils of the day. He approached Hatch and stood six inches taller than her. He said nothing. His face might as well have been etched in stone as Hatch met his gaze. He looked at Hatch and then to the open gate. His silent command to move had been given. Hatch took it and left.

She headed back up the trail and around the bend, disappearing behind the thick mass of tree trunks lining the road. Hatch entered the Jeep; Ben still in the passenger seat.

"Let me guess. Nothing?"

"We'll see." Hatch put the SUV into drive and turned back toward the main road. "I've been invited back tomorrow."

Before turning left and heading back into town, Hatch pulled her phone from the satchel she'd carried. She pulled up the photo she'd snapped unbeknownst to The Shepherd. Taken at an odd angle, it captured the face of the Eternal Light's leader. She sent it to Jordan Tracy in the hopes that with the assets at his disposal he would be capable of finding an identification for the mysterious preacher. And with it maybe some insight into the questions The Shepherd had dodged.

One thing was certain, by morning's light tomorrow, Hatch hoped to have a much clearer picture of things in Jericho Falls.

EIGHTEEN

Savage and Thorpe had spent the last several hours in The Cave, going over the years of case history. They found no tangible evidence connecting to Glenn Miller. Savage was flipping through the pages of a report he'd already read, hoping to find a breadcrumb of connective tissue to his case, when the phone on Thorpe's desk rang.

Thorpe moved a stack of papers, blocking his reach, and picked up the receiver. "When? Why am I just now hearing about this? I want the full report immediately. Assign the case to me." Thorpe hung up the phone.

"What is it?" Savage asked.

"A girl aged twelve went missing two days ago."

"Two days ago? Why are you just hearing about it now?"

"Apparently, the deputy on patrol had tagged it as a civil case over child custody, and he was looking at the father, but his sergeant changed it."

"Where?"

"Small town called Jericho Falls. About forty-five minutes from here, probably thirty the way I drive." Thorpe said.

"Mind if I tag along? It's been a while since I've had a partner." Savage asked.

"Me too."

The two men left the cave and the crude drawing of the Twister Man and set out for Jericho Falls.

SAVAGE RODE SHOTGUN in Thorpe's Chevy suburban. The sun set as they made their way west. The night sky was coated with the swirling of angry gray clouds.

"Tell me more about McKenzie Blackmore and her encounter with the Twister Man."

"Her family lives just north of here in a trailer park on the outskirts of Lebanon. McKenzie had snuck out to play in the rain, as children do. She had not wandered far from her home. Her father didn't realize she left, and when he called her for dinner and she didn't respond, he went outside to look for her. Stepping to the porch, he called out to her, but the wind had already begun to howl. He stepped back inside to grab a flashlight to search for her, but above the howl he heard the scream."

"Besides the drawing, was McKenzie able to give you anything in the way of a description?"

"She said he looked like a tree. Her father had grabbed a shotgun, and he set out to find his daughter. He saw her lifted in the air. The man carrying her was barely visible. Her father took aim with the shotgun and fired. His daughter fell to the ground. The man disappeared before her father got a look. The tornado warnings had already sounded. It was too dangerous to chase him into the woods."

"If the father got a shot off, did he hit the kidnapper?"

"He said he believed so. It looked as though after he had dropped McKenzie that he ran with a limp."

"Was there any evidence, blood or otherwise?"

Thorpe shook his head no while keeping his eyes on the road. "Ever been through a tornado?"

"Can't say that I have."

"Well, let me tell you, from an investigative standpoint, it's an evidence eradicator. I couldn't even find a pellet of a bird shot that he'd said he'd fired. No DNA, no trace evidence."

"But a story you believe?"

Thorpe nodded. "With all my heart. The notes from this police report gave the location of the Eternal Light commune."

Thorpe slowed as the GPS showed they'd arrived, and he almost passed the entrance in the darkness. He hit the brakes and turned left, taking a dirt road, and following it to its end at the gated entrance, now closed. Savage and Thorpe left the vehicle as rain began to fall.

Thorpe knocked on the gate. They could see the smoke rising above the fence from campfires. Nobody came. There were voices on the other side, distant and indiscernible. Thorpe knocked louder.

"Wilson County Sheriff's Office. Can someone please come to the gate?"

A shadow blocked out the light seeping through the gap between the gate and the fence. The man standing inside was about Savage's height, maybe a few inches taller. The shadow cast from the fence hid the details of his face.

"Excuse me, I'm Detective Jim Thorpe with Wilson County Sheriff's Office. We'd like to speak with you about Kyla Green."

No response came from the other side.

"Did you hear what I said?"

There was a sound, like the rustle of dried leaves, and then through the slit where the shadowed man stood came a piece of paper. Thorpe took it and read it.

"Leave."

He pocketed the paper. "Maybe you didn't hear me. I'm Detective Jim Thorpe with the Wilson County Sheriff's Office. I'm here to speak with Dorothy Green, Kyla's mother."

The man beyond the fence gate shifted out of view and disappeared from sight.

"What do you make of that?" Savage said. "Not very welcoming for a bunch of holy rollers."

"Well, it's not like I can ram through the gate."

"Maybe we'll have better luck in the morning."

The rain grew steadier, and the two retreated to Thorpe's suburban. "Not sure what you have for accommodations, but I live about thirty-five minutes from here in the direction we just came. It's small, but the couch is pretty comfortable. I don't think my wife would mind."

"I don't want to be a bother. Is there a motel nearby?"

"There's only one in Jericho Falls. Otherwise, we're going about twenty miles out of the way."

"Sounds like I'm staying in Jericho Falls."

"Suit yourself."

Thorpe pulled onto the main road and made his way into town. They drove by a restaurant called Clem's.

"If you're hungry, good food. Eaten there a time or two over the years. My treat."

"I had an early start, and it sounds like we're going to get an early start tomorrow, too. I think I'll just take my chances with a vending machine tonight."

Thorpe drove him to the motel. They said goodbye with the agreement that Thorpe would return in the morning, and after breakfast, the two would head back to make a second attempt to contact Kyla's mother.

Savage got a key to room number seven. As he walked to his room, he took note of the two cars in the lot. Out of force of habit, he touched the hoods of the cars as he passed them. The sedan parked in front of room one was cold. He touched the hood of the Jeep as he passed it. It was warm. Old habits die hard.

The light in room three was on as Savage passed and made his way to his temporary quarters. As he entered the small, but surprisingly clean room, the image of the girl's crudely drawn Twister Man came to his mind. He wondered if the eyes hidden behind the gray swirls were that of Glen Miller's or somebody else's, and he hoped that tomorrow would bring the answer.

NINETEEN

HATCH WOKE EARLY AND HEADED OUT THE DOOR. DARKNESS STILL clung to the world outside as she made her way from the curb to her Jeep. Jordan Tracy still had not gotten back to her with any information on the photograph she'd sent. His brother's room was still dark minus the white light from the television, which Hatch assumed he'd left on while sleeping. She made her way out with soft steps, hoping to avoid any request to join her for this morning's outing to the Eternal Light's commune.

The only light beyond what seeped out into the dark through Ben's drawn shade came from the dim bulb above the main office's front door. Though she craved a cup, Hatch decided to forgo the coffee, hoping that bypassing Harlin's morning brew would help her avoid any prying by the town's gossip, as he was so named by the friendly restaurant owner. That hope was dashed when the door popped open.

"You're off to an early start," Harlin stood halfway out, propping the door open with the side of his boot.

"Only way to catch the worms." Hatch opened the driver's side door and tossed her satchel onto the passenger seat.

"I can make you a cup to go if you like?" He jutted his chin in the direction of the office. "It's no trouble, really."

The dark sky grew brighter with each passing minute. With sunrise just around the corner, Hatch politely declined Harlin's offer and climbed inside the Cherokee. She pulled away from the motel, the crackle and pop of the rocks underneath marked her departure. Harlin remained in the doorway to his office, watching her until she was out of sight.

Hatch sped through town. Most of the lights in the trailer homes and small ranches were off. As she passed by the diner, Clem could be seen through the glass of the front door. He was busy serving a couple early-risers bellied up to the counter.

The Jeep scooted past the edge of the town square and onward until she passed the distinctive red of Clem's mailbox. Less than two minutes later, Hatch reached the dirt road to the Eternal Light commune.

She looked to the sky as she rounded the bend toward the main gate. Gauging the growing brightness to the east, she figured she had ten minutes before the sun would be up. In the military, raids and ambushes were planned for this time of day. The advantages were many. Night watchmen were at their weariest and the subtle shift from dark to light messed with their vision, making it a prime time for attack. Though the purpose of her visit had no tactical element, she felt the rush that comes in those moments before battle as she made her way to the open gate. Standing in wait at the entrance was Dorothy Green, Kyla's mother, and her small Scottie stood guard by her ankle.

Hatch parked the Jeep and approached. "I'm here for this morning's ceremony."

"I know." Green looked to the satchel slung over Hatch's shoulder. "You must set aside your bag before you can enter. You can have nothing with you when you enter for this morning's Rise."

Hatch put her cellphone in the satchel and then jogged back to her rental and tossed it on the seat before returning.

Green held out her arms. A white tunic was draped across them. "You may leave your clothes on but must cover yourself with this if you wish to participate in the Rise."

"Participate? I thought I was invited to watch." Hatch accepted the tunic.

"We are all here to watch over her and bear witness to the transcendence at hand." Green's voice was low and had an emptiness to it.

Beneath piety, Hatch saw the deep pain of a grieving mother as she assisted in pulling the tunic over Hatch's head. The sleeves were cut wide, allowing for a full range of motion. The fabric hung loosely over her clothes, ending just above the ankles. Hatch noticed that Green's did also. As Hatch took stock of the group, she realized that all the women wore longer tunics than their male counterparts.

The wind began to blow and Hatch's dress fluttered about. Green moved with the grace of a ballerina as she stepped behind Hatch and wrapped a braided rope around her waist. She gave a light tug, drawing in the waist and bringing the flapping to an end. Hatch felt the gentleness in her touch, and thought, without knowing, that Dorothy Green must be a wonderful mother.

Before they made their way further into the interior of the commune and while Green was still close by, Hatch whispered, "I'm here to help you find your daughter."

Green reared back as if Hatch had just slapped her. The solemn serenity was replaced by fear. Green shot a worried glance behind her to where the others had gathered, stopping on one person in particular, the leader of the Eternal Light.

The Shepherd stood beside a stone altar holding his staff. Laying on the granite slab was Marigold. The little girl's hair was braided, just as it had been the day before. Around her head lay a wreath of flowers.

The others were seated in a tight circle around the altar. They sat cross-legged with their hands resting on their knees. It was silent, minus the rustling leaves.

As Green escorted Hatch, she whispered, "There is no talking during the ceremony. You must be silent during the Rise."

Green approached a gap in the circle where space had been set aside for her return with Hatch. Mathias sat just behind The Shepherd. His tall form stood out among the shorter members.

The Shepherd stood motionless, except for the breeze flapping the bottom edges of his tunic. His eyes were transfixed on the girl before him. The first beams of sunlight began to crest a distant ridgeline. As time passed and the sun continued to rise, the group remained silent, focusing on the child covered in flowers.

Hatch looked at the girl and thought again of Daphne sleeping next to her in her sister's bed.

Marigold was Sleeping Beauty incarnate. Her eyes closed, her hands remained folded across her chest. Her body was covered in fresh flowers, the white of her tunic peeking through.

The sunlight cleared the treetops and danced its way across the low rooftops of the two rows of houses until it reached the altar. Inch by inch, the light kissed the girl's skin, starting with her toes and working its way up the length of her body until the altar and the girl on it were bathed in light. Colorful flowers showed their true beauty in the morning's glow. Hatch wondered if the little Marigold had picked them all herself.

The Shepherd raised his staff high, turning it sideways over the length of the girl's body, the etched infinity symbols catching the morning light.

"We bear witness to Marigold's transcendence, her Rise from girl to woman. She now possesses God's greatest gift, taken for granted in the world outside these walls. Her womb now ready, when the time is right, she will take on the greatest calling. Motherhood. The womb is the key to God's eternal light. For it is from there His likeness is born, like the passing of a torch to light a dark path, a path to eternity, one without end. Rise, young Marigold, and let us bathe in your eternal light."

Marigold sat up, sending a cascade of flowers to the dirt around the altar. Her eyes opened. She blinked them against the brightness of the sun. Then she stood on the altar and opened her arms wide. The childlike wonder that Hatch had seen when she first met the girl was there.

Marigold then placed her hands on her stomach and said, "I will pass the torch."

The group raised their hands in praise and called out in unison, "Light Eternal."

The Shepherd brought his staff down. "We have borne witness, and now we must celebrate."

Hatch could still feel the sadness emanating from Green, who stood beside her. The missing girl's mother forced a smile as she raised her arms in worship.

Moving like a conga line in a serpentine fashion, the group snaked the figure eight around the altar where Marigold danced happily among the fallen flowers. The group broke into song as the procession continued. Hatch moved with the flow, keeping step with Green, who was now in front of her. She didn't sing or raise her hands like the others, but she did bear witness, not only to the young girl but the man who stood by with staff in hand, watching Marigold with intensity.

Hatch moved with the flow, looking for an opportunity to further press Green on her daughter's disappearance but finding none. The followers were too closely packed and The Shepherd, when his eyes weren't on Marigold, were on Hatch.

The dancing and celebration continued. Fires were lit in the stone pits scattered throughout. Several men and woman began preparing food for a feast to be served later that morning. Children and adults alike danced and laughed as they went about their work. If Kyla's disappearance wasn't hanging over this commune like a black cloud, Hatch might've even enjoyed herself.

Above the celebration, Hatch heard the rumble of tires coming down the path. She felt her stomach drop and turned, expecting to see the beat-up sedan belonging to Ben Tracy and surprised to see an SUV instead. And not just any old kind. In the front grill of the Chevy Suburban, Hatch could make out the red and blue of the strobe lights contained within. With sun rays bouncing off the windshield, she couldn't make out either the driver or the passenger in the approaching SUV.

The vehicle came to a stop just outside the open gate. A man with wire-rimmed glasses and a mustache, wearing a light green sweater vest and slacks, stepped out. Hatch could see a side arm and badge on his hip, confirming her earlier observation.

His partner then exited from the passenger side. Hatch stopped dead in her tracks, causing the young woman walking behind her to bump into her and to dump the basket of freshly dug potatoes she'd been carrying onto the ground.

Hatch apologized and bent to help the woman pick up the loose potatoes. Her heart was still beating erratically at the sight of Dalton Savage. Her mind, moments before sharply tuned to members of the commune and The Shepherd in particular, was now doing its best to remember how to breathe. Savage was approaching. She could tell he hadn't yet picked her out of the crowd. Not sure whether to run from him or to him, she did neither. After helping retrieve the potatoes, Hatch stood frozen in place.

The Shepherd stepped beside Hatch. "Why would you invite others to this day's ceremony?"

"I didn't."

"At Marigold's request or not, I need to ask you to leave." The expressive tone that he'd used when delivering his sermon was all but gone. Dorothy appeared and retrieved the tunic that she'd lent Hatch. Hatch met Dorothy's eyes. Without speaking, Hatch pleaded to the woman to tell her something, but Dorothy hurried off as Savage and his partner approached.

Hatch walked towards him. Savage did a double take and then his eyes went wide. She saw the question forming on his lips, but gave a subtle shake of her head. He closed his mouth and continued to walk in the direction of The Shepherd.

As Hatch passed Savage, she whispered, "I'll be at Clem's when you're done."

He slowed to a stop and fumbled with the words in his mouth. He was rendered speechless and offered nothing but a confused nod. Hatch continued on toward the Jeep parked beyond the gate and didn't break stride. She'd smelled the licorice on Savage as she passed. It took everything in her power not to look back.

TWENTY

Savage looked back at Hatch as she walked away to the Jeep and got inside without so much as a glance back in his direction. The surprise and elation of seeing her had been dampened by the coldness in their exchange. He had a thousand questions for her percolating in his mind, but those would have to wait.

"A friend of yours?" Thorpe said.

"Something like that."

The man with long hair and a staff who'd been talking to Hatch as they'd arrived closed the distance on Savage and Thorpe, stopping them from meeting the celebrants who were scurrying about the common area.

Fires burned and large pots boiled. A lamb was being turned on a spit, sending the scent of the cooked meat into the air. In spite of the merriment of song and dance, Savage felt the unwanted glances of those dressed in white.

"Sir, I'm Detective Thorpe with Wilson County Sheriff's Office. This here is Sherriff Savage from Hawk's Landing, Colorado."

The Shepherd looked Savage up and down, resting his eyes on the silver of his badge that peeked out from an untucked button-down shirt. "What brings you all the way from Colorado?"

"Closure."

"Ah, something many seek but never find. In life or in death." The Shepherd held firmly to the staff in his hand and delivered the words with sermon-like reverence.

Thorpe cleared his throat. "Sir, we'd like to speak to Dorothy Green about the disappearance of her daughter, Kyla."

"We do not recognize those names here, but I know of whom you speak. The mother has taken the name Wind Walker. And her daughter is known within these walls as Moon Dancer."

"Why the name change?" Savage asked.

"Fresh start. Everybody deserves one by the Lord's grace." The Shepherd looked to his people. "Each takes a name that calls to them. Wind Walker arrived during tornadic winds."

"And Moon Dancer, how did that come about?" Thorpe had a pad and pen at the ready.

"She is a child of the night. Often I've found her wandering far from here in the dark hours."

"Where does she go when wandering?" Savage looked out at the expanse of the rise and fall of the wooded land surrounding them.

The Shepherd shrugged. "Belies asking. To wander explains much. But I'd say the stream that runs beyond the homes was a favorite of hers. On more than one occasion, I've found her out by the small falls that feed the stream. She loved to watch the moon dance along the water."

"Can you show us?" Thorpe adjusted his glasses as he looked up from his pad.

"I'm sorry to say, but no. Not today."

"There's a little girl who's missing. I think that trumps any celebration you might have planned." Savage let the edge in his voice be heard. Thorpe shot a glance in his direction.

"Maybe you are right, but we believe differently here. Celebration of light always pushes away the dark. This morning's celebration will reach the heavens. And in doing so, will call forth His angels to bring our daughter of the light home to her flock."

"I don't think that's going to have the effect you think it is." Savage stepped closer to the religious leader. "Your best bet is to let us look around, talk to each member of your flock and get a clear picture of what happened to Kyla Green."

The Shepherd dropped his feigned smile into a frown. "I think we've been more than accommodating. One of your deputies has already taken his report."

"Well, that's why we're here now." Thorpe tried to match Savage's confidence, but it came out flat.

"We've given all the information we have. Nothing has changed since then, and her mother does not wish to speak to you."

"Can I get your legal name for my report?"

"I am The Shepherd, and this is my flock."

"Well, you've lost one of your sheep," Savage said.

"We have cooperated with you to the extent we are willing. We are now turning our voices to God so that He may call her home to us. If there is nothing further, and you gentlemen do not have an order from the court, then I'm going to kindly ask you to leave." A tall, thin man wearing similar garb moved beside The Shepherd. "Mathias will see you out."

Savage looked at Mathias and recognized him as last night's gate-keeper. Mathias raised his left hand, guiding them back toward the open gate and their vehicle parked just beyond.

"He's right. There's not much we can really do," Thorpe whispered to Savage as they turned to leave.

Savage sighed in frustration, and just before turning to follow Thorpe, directed one last question at The Shepherd. "What can you tell me about Glenn Miller?"

Savage noticed a slight tremble in the tall Mathias's outstretched hand before he dropped it to his side and cast a look at the Shepherd. The Shepherd shot a look behind him at his followers, none of whom appeared to have heard the question.

The Shepherd stepped closer with his etched staff. "We do not speak the names of the departed here."

"Even if it means protecting a murderer?" Savage focused intently on The Shepherd's reaction to the question. The holy leader was definitely caught off-guard by it. Figuring out what that meant was the tricky part. "Would it matter if I told you the person he killed was a little girl?"

"Actually, there are a total of two we know of and probably countless more." Thorpe turned his attention back to The Shepherd.

The Shepherd looked to Mathias and sighed. His head drooped a bit as he spoke. "Glen Miller was my Shepherd. He pulled me out of darkness and brought me into the light."

"What do you mean *your* Shepherd?" Savage asked.

The Shepherd spoke now in a whisper. "I am breaking one of our cardinal rules in speaking to you about this, but I do so to honor the lives of those victims. I was not always the man you see before you. Miller was my psychologist who brought me out of a very dark place after tragedy and addiction had ravaged my soul. The Eternal Light was born from our therapy sessions, and he was our founder."

"What happened? Why did he leave?"

"His interpretation of the word became muddied."

"How do you mean?"

The Shepherd turned to Mathias, who stood by his side like a silent sentinel. "Open your mouth, my son."

Mathias opened his mouth. Where a tongue should be was only a misshapen nub. Mathias closed his mouth.

"Miller removed his tongue." The Shepherd said.

"Why?" Savage asked.

"A question to which I have no answer. Mathias has never chosen to speak of it, and he has faced his forced virtue with unmatched resilience."

"What happened after?"

"Miller was asked to leave."

"And it wasn't reported to the authorities?"

"No. That is not our way." The Shepherd paused, momentarily lost in thought, and then asked, "Where is he now?"

"Dead. Somebody decided not to remain silent." Savage thought of Billy Graver and the violence he'd used to scream his truth.

"If Miller is dead, what connection is there to our little Moon Dancer?" The Shepherd asked.

"That's what we're trying to find out." Savage said.

"I wish there was more that I could tell you."

"I do too." Savage turned and he and Thorpe headed back to their vehicle.

"How fast can you type a search warrant?" Savage asked once they were outside of the gates and the earshot of the tall, tongueless Mathias.

"I may not be great on my feet in an interview, but paperwork I can do." Thorpe gave a sheepish smile. "To answer your question. Fast. Why?"

"Because I want to come back here and comb every inch of that place until I find the truth about what happened to that little girl. Because right now, I'm having a hell of a time connecting the dots."

Thorpe drove Savage back into town. When they reached Clem's diner, Savage asked him to stop. Thorpe saw Hatch inside. "Got a hot date with that reporter?"

"Something along those lines."

"I'm going to head back to the office to start putting that search warrant together," Thorpe said before driving off.

Savage took a moment to look at Hatch before entering the diner. He felt the old embers begin to burn bright as he watched her.

TWENTY-ONE

HATCH SAT IN THE SAME BOOTH SHE AND BEN HAD SHARED THE previous morning. The restaurant was packed with locals and Clem was busy tending to them. He'd stopped by her table when she first arrived. Hatch said she was waiting for someone and would wait to order. Clem had been by once more to top off her cup.

She placed a call to Jordan Tracy to check if he had any luck with the picture she'd sent. He'd said he was still working on it. Although Talon had a unique set of assets at its disposal, facial recognition software wasn't the thirty-second turnaround people saw on TV. The reality was, it took time, and she still had nothing on The Shepherd.

After receiving a second text message from Cruise asking, *Everything okay?* Hatch had responded, *Still working some leads. Don't have to worry about me. I'm just another pair of eyes on the ground, hoping to put some pieces together.*

Hitting send on the message, she hoped it would satiate his concern.

Instead, he fired back an immediate response. *Do you need anything from me? I'll come out.*

No need. Will be sharing my information with the investigators handling the case. Once we figure out what's going on, the ball will be in their court.

Hatch left out the part that one of those investigators happened to be Dalton Savage.

Will you be back in time for Taylor's service in two days?

I'll try.

The door to the restaurant opened as she hit send on her last message. Savage scanned the room. At seeing him, Hatch felt her heart rate increase. His presence had an uncanny effect on her.

Making eye contact, he gave a half smile as he walked in her direction. He slid into the seat across from her, exhaling as he sat. The hint of black licorice carried on his breath.

"You're the last person I expected to see here." Savage said.

"I could say the same," Hatch replied. "We didn't connect during our phone tag."

"I didn't mean to be a bother," Savage said as Clem approached with a fresh pot of coffee.

"I see you've made a new friend," Clem said.

"Actually, he's an old one," Hatch said.

Clem topped Hatch's coffee mug off and then filled the one in front of Savage. "You a tin man?" Clem asked.

"Come again?" Savage looked up at the restaurant owner, his milk white mustache drawn up in a smile.

"I caught a glimpse of your badge when you entered. Never seen you before. Are you with the county or the state?"

"Neither. Hawk's Landing, Colorado."

"You picked a heck of a time to come to Jericho Falls. You're smack dab in the middle of tornado season. Keep an eye out for the warnings. The watch is already up."

On the small TV set in the corner of the restaurant, Hatch had been reading the closed captions on the bottom while she waited for Savage. The Storm Prediction Center had issued a severe weather threat across Central Tennessee.

The SPC had stated the atmosphere was unstable and tornados had the potential to materialize ahead of an approaching cold front. They stated that the moisture and wind shear mixed with the cold mid-level temperatures could form super cells. The newscaster went on to say that the SPC had been late in last March's warning, which led to a tornado outbreak that cost the lives of twenty-five people.

"I'll be prepping the restaurant a little later. When these things hit, they come on fast. If you hear the warning, you all take shelter. Hear me? Don't get caught out in it."

"Will do," Hatch said.

The time was somewhere between lunch and dinner. Hatch stuck with the shepherd's pie, and Savage decided to join her.

"Well, looks like you two got some catching up to do. Be back with your food."

Clem moved through the restaurant with the pot of coffee and disappeared into the kitchen area.

"I don't know where to start," Savage said.

"How are the kids?"

"Jake is practicing his martial arts every day. He's got his heart set on wearing a badge in the future."

"I can think of no better calling for him." Remembering the bravery Jake had shown when an armed intruder had entered her childhood home. He fought to protect his sister, Hatch's mother, and Hatch herself. "How's Daphne?"

The mention of her young niece's name brought a smile to Savage's face and seemed to work at reducing the tension between them.

"That little one is a rainbow in motion. She is becoming quite the artist. Heck, my office walls are covered with her work and there's a new drawing just about every time I stop over."

"You still check in on them?"

"Always. Plus, your mom's got me addicted to her coffee, so there's that."

"How is she?"

Hatch and her mother had a tenuous relationship at best. After the years apart, the rift between them had barely begun to heal when Hatch had to leave home again.

"Jasmine's doing great. I don't know if it's my place to say, but she is seeing someone."

Hatch's eyes popped wide. The thought of her mother with anybody but her father, even in the twenty years since his murder, caught her off guard.

"Really?"

The smile remained on Savage's face. "You won't believe me when I tell you who it is."

"Are you going to make me guess?"

"I don't think you would if I gave you all the time in the world. Jed Russell."

Hatch thought of the old recluse who had come to Hatch's aid and proven himself worthy in battle. There are few greater tests of a person's resolve, and Hatch had borne witness to it firsthand. She trusted Jed with her life. Somehow, it seemed fitting to entrust him with the care of her mother.

"Is she happy?"

"Happier than I've seen her in a very long time."

"Good."

"I thought you would've been back by now to see for yourself."

Hatch thought about how she had left things with Savage, how she had finally cleared her name, yet she hadn't returned.

"I meant to, but it's complicated."

"Seems like everything with you is."

"I've got to clear some things personally before I can come back. Just because my name is clear doesn't mean my head is. And right now, I think we have more important things to talk about than my absence."

"Like why you're here?" Savage asked, "And why you're wearing a reporter's badge?"

"The father of the missing girl, Kyla Green, happens to be the brother of my commander at Talon. I'm doing this as a favor."

"And what is it you're doing, exactly?"

"I'm eyes and ears on the ground. I'm here to help."

"By interfering with an investigation?"

"I think you know me better than that. I'm not interfering. I'm assisting."

"Assisting how?"

"By gaining access where you can't."

"Like this morning at that ceremony?"

"Exactly. And yesterday, when I met with and interviewed The Shepherd."

"Were you able to get a name on him?"

"No. I forwarded a photo, hoping that facial recognition will turn something up."

"Why don't we compare notes and see where we're at?"

"Well, I know she went missing two days ago. The community is tight-lipped and controlled by The Shepherd."

"We saw that firsthand. He refused to let us speak to Kyla's mother."

"I tried to speak with her this morning at the ceremony."

"Did you get anything from her?"

"No, except that she was scared and worried. It was in her eyes."

"The Shepherd is a bit of an enigma, hard to read him."

"How does this case connect to Hawk's Landing, is my question?"

"That's why I called you."

She heard the dejection in Savage's voice. "Yeah. I'm sorry about that. I meant to get back to you, but—"

Savage waved a hand, dismissing Hatch's excuse before she gave it. "Had me rattled, is all. I've seen plenty of death, but this one really threw me. A teenager, barely a man, walked into the grocery and emptied a gun into the back of a seventy-two-year-old man."

"Why?"

"The boy is Billy Graver. He was abducted, along with his sister, several years back. About a week later, Billy was found walking out of a cave in the woods, covered in his sister's blood. Being autistic and unable to communicate, he spent the rest of his time in and out of mental health intensive care. Add in the trauma of whatever he witnessed...He escaped from the facility and killed Glenn Miller in front of several people. After a bit of digging and some legwork, the spotlight of my investigation turned from Graver to Miller himself.

We found a grave near Miller's home. Buried in it, the bones of Graver's sister Amanda were found."

"I still don't see the connection to here, Jericho Falls, and the missing Kyla Green."

"I'm getting there. In the grave, forensics found human bones and was able to match it to the DNA of a missing girl from ten years ago, from here in Wilson County. Detective Thorpe has been working it for almost the entirety of those ten years and found a pattern of disappearances."

"Are we talking about a serial case?"

"The worst kind, involving children. All the missing are around the age of twelve, all female, all disappearing before or during a major storm event."

"But if Miller's dead, then..."

"That's the thing that's bugging us. I've got a little information."

"What's the connection?"

"Glenn Miller was the founder of the Eternal Light."

Hatch thought of the interview she had with The Shepherd and how he had spoken of his mentor, of his Shepherd.

"Maybe Miller passed on more than his teachings."

TWENTY-TWO

KYLA ROLLED TO HER SIDE. THE BALES OF HAY COVERED BY ONLY A sheet crunched and crackled under her light frame, small bits of the rough straw poked at her skin. As uncomfortable as it was, it was still better than the dirt floor. The room was dark, except for the dim candlelight. The flame cast shadows around the mud walls. Kyla had nightmares about the things cast by the light, none more terrifying than her captor.

The walls of the small room were made of packed mud. Thick support beams were set at each of the corners and held in place the wooden boards above that stretched across the ceiling. The half-eaten loaf of bread and empty cup of water serving as her only forms of nourishment, sat on the nearby nightstand.

A heavy wooden door sealed her inside. The heavy door brace set against the outside had made it impossible for Kyla to open it. Long past the ability to form tears, the passage of time no longer seemed comprehendible. Kyla tried to measure how long she'd been in captivity, but without a window, she had lost all reference for day and night. Being resourceful was something her mother prided in her. And keeping her in mind, Kyla calculated her incarceration by the meals left for her. The bread and water beside her bed had been her sixth meal since she'd been shoved in here.

On the far wall, a large Newton's Cradle sat on a slender wooden desk. The balls clacked loudly. She was given specific instructions never to let it stop. Afraid of what consequences would befall her, Kyla complied. No matter how hard she pressed her palms to her ears, the clacking penetrated incessantly.

As she tucked her knees tight against her chest, curling herself into a fetal position and turning away from the cradle, Kyla stared at the brown wall nearest her and tried desperately to call up a memory of her father. She tried to picture his face again. It had been seven long years since she'd seen him.

When they'd gone into the Eternal Light, all possessions had been left at the gate, including photographs. As time passed, she found it harder to draw up a memory of her father's face. In the darkness, she forced herself to call forward the last good day she could remember with him.

She was five when he had taken the training wheels off her bike. He had coached her through what to do. Remembering being terrified, she held the handlebars with a death grip. She remembered her dad's hands gently holding her at the shoulders.

She remembered what he said, whispering in her ear just before he pushed her forward. "Ride like the wind."

She remembered the calming sounds of his footsteps as he jogged alongside her. Could hear his voice cheering her as she picked up speed, and the wind blew through her hair.

That night in Augusta was the last one they were a family. The last night everything in her life was whole. In celebrating her victory over the training wheels, her father had snuck Kyla up to the rooftop of their apartment where they lived. He set up a small grill where they roasted marshmallows.

When they'd had their fill of sweets, she and her father lay snuggled on a sleeping bag he'd set out for them. They lay beneath the clear Georgia night sky and stared up at the stars.

They spent what felt like an eternity in each other's embrace while her father pointed out the different constellations. Her favorite had been the hunter Orion, primarily because it was easiest to pick out. The three stars that formed the fabled hunter's belt were much like the belt she wore now, though she felt less like a hunter and more like prey.

That one memory, cherished above all others, was the reason Kyla took the name Moon Dancer when her mom had brought her to the Eternal Light. And it was that memory that sent her wandering each night, hoping along the way she would find her father among those stars.

Kyla remembered that day and night like it was yesterday, but for the life of her couldn't call her father's face to mind. Closing her eyes, she tried to picture his face, but the years had blurred it.

She wondered if she'd recognize her dad should she ever see him again. Looking around her, she felt less hopeful with every meal served. She longed to hear his footsteps running alongside her one more time.

A door banged closed outside her cell. Fear crept in, amplified by the rhythmic clacking of the cradle. Kyla forced her mind back to the rooftop, back to the stars, and she silently called out to the great hunter, praying he would come to her rescue and wanting nothing more than to feel her father's gentle hands guiding her, protecting her, once again. But she felt nothing but the weight of her life bearing down on her small shoulders.

Kyla held her breath and tucked deeper under her thin covers as footsteps that moved in sync with the clack of the balls came to a stop outside her door.

TWENTY-THREE

AFTER FINISHING THEIR MEAL, AND AFTER SAVAGE HAD TOLD HATCH, Thorpe's story of the Twister Man, they had spent the afternoon helping Clem and some of the neighboring businesses in boarding up windows and doors in preparation of the coming storm. Clem compensated their kindness by giving Hatch the fresh batch of corn-bread that sat boxed and wrapped on the rear seat of the Jeep as Hatch and Savage rode back to the motel.

Savage had called Thorpe and relayed the information Hatch had provided. Hatch parked in front of her room. The dark sky was now littered with thick, ominous clouds swirling menacingly. A light rain had begun to fall, and the winds had picked up. A heavy gust blew the door wide as Hatch opened it. The two stood in front of Hatch's room.

"Thorpe's working on a search warrant, and he should have it by morning. If Kyla Green is somewhere in that commune, we'll find her."

"Morning is a long time away." Hatch looked at the raging storm clouds.

"I can't just go kicking the gate door in. You know how it works."

"Yes, I do."

"I see that look in your eye, Hatch. Let Thorpe do his job. If there's merit to this, then the search warrant will prove it. And then, any evidence won't be tainted by the fruit of the poisonous tree."

Hatch knew the rules. They were the same for a military police officer as they were for their civilian counterparts. Evidence of a crime obtained outside the proper channels was often dismissed.

The fourth amendment search and seizure laws were in place to protect an individual's right to privacy, one held firm by the highest courts in the land. Hatch knew better than to press.

"I'm going to head to my room. I've got to update my side. I'll let you know if I've got anything worth adding to your warrant."

Savage stepped close, the boxed cornbread the only divider between their personal space. The wind wafted the sweet scent of the box's contents in the air around them. The tension between them was as thick as the cornmeal used to bind the treat.

"It tore my heart in two when you left Hawk's Landing."

"I never meant to."

Savage shook his head. "No, don't. Seeing you now makes the ache worse. Look, Hatch, I don't know where we stand at the end of this."

"Let's see where things are when the dust settles."

Looking at his lips, she thought of the kiss on the mountaintop interrupted by the snake's bite. Here they were, face to face, separated by air and opportunity. Both barriers seemed impassable.

She could feel Savage's longing. Not wanting to further complicate an already complicated situation, she offered him an awkward smile that did little to ease the strain in his eyes as she said goodnight.

Savage held out the box in his hand.

"You keep it," she said. "I think I've had my fill of cornbread for the day."

"See you in the morning. Hopefully with a search warrant. Goodnight."

Savage turned and headed to his room. Hatch entered hers, casting a quick glance at Savage's back as he walked away before closing the door to the howling wind. Picking up her cell, she called Jordan Tracy.

"Good timing. I was just about to call you," Tracy said.

She relayed the information from her conversation with Savage, and the status of the pending search warrant.

"Well, you can put a name on that search warrant."

"You identified The Shepherd?"

"I did. Your Shepherd is a man by the name of Samuel Cantrell."

"What did you find?"

"He comes from money. His family made a killing in the California wine market."

This supported what The Shepherd had told her about having funds at his disposal to buy the land outright.

"Apparently, he had everything going for him. He was a three sport All-American athlete, and besides the wealth of his family, he was looking at several full ride scholarships for football. During his senior year, he was in a car crash that damaged his right leg and ended any chance of him playing at the college level."

"That explains the walking staff."

"There's more. I found an article on the crash. He had a passenger with him at the time, his sister."

"Was she hurt?"

"She was killed."

"How old?"

"Twelve. After the crash, he got into drugs. He'd spent multiple years in and out of rehab, and it looks as though he just up and disappeared about fifteen years ago, completely off the grid."

And like that, everything made sense to Hatch. The dots now connected.

"I know what you're thinking, but this isn't our fight, Hatch. Let the authorities handle it from here. If The Shepherd is our guy, let law enforcement take him down the right way."

"Morning might be too late."

Just then, the deafening wail of a siren filled the air.

"What was that?" Tracy said.

"Tornado warning. The storm is here. Time is up."

"What are you going to do?"

"What I do best." Hatch ended the call.

Throwing on a windbreaker, she left the room. Savage's door was still closed. She hustled to her Jeep. As she opened the door, a voice came in over the wind.

"Wherever you're going, count me in." She turned to see Ben Tracy standing outside of his door and moving towards Hatch. "It's not safe. And it's my daughter."

Hatch couldn't find an argument worth having, and time was wasting.

"Get in."

He took up the passenger seat as Hatch hopped into the driver's seat. Harlin exploded out of the main office, a frenzied look on his face, calling to Hatch.

"You two best not be heading out in this storm. These things come in fast and hard, and from nowhere. You'll never see it coming. My main office has a shelter underneath. Come with me."

"I can't."

Hatch offered no further explanation. She backed out and headed away from the motel, back to the main road. Just as she cleared the gravel of the lot, the door to Savage's room swung open. Backlit by the light inside stood the Hawk's Landing sheriff.

She looked at his face in the rearview mirror, hoping to see it again when the storm was over. She could see he was calling out to her, but she heard nothing above the roar of the car engine, the howl of the wind, and the siren playing in the backdrop.

Hatch sped through town, seeing only one truck parked in front of Clem's restaurant. She glimpsed Clem himself between one of the boarded windows, still inside, apparently choosing to weather the storm in the place where he spent most of his life. Leaving town behind, she made her way to the commune. As she came to Clem Johnson's red mailbox, she turned into his driveway.

"Where are you going?" Ben said with a look of concern.

"There's a break in the fence along the stream that runs between the properties."

"How do you know?"

"It's where Clem last saw your daughter."

Hatch pulled to a stop behind Clem's ranch, parking in wet grass. Hopping out, she jogged toward the wood line. Ben wheezed as he attempted to keep up.

They came to the stream a few minutes later and found the gap in the fence only a few feet between the end of the fence and the stream bed. The fence line picked up on the other side.

As the rain intensified, the clouds above began spinning. The town's siren could barely be heard above the wind as it sounded its warning cry once again. Hatch moved through the uneven terrain, passing through the trees and making her way towards the row of houses serving as the main living space for the Eternal Light followers.

As she came up along the backside of the row of wooden houses, it looked like a ghost town. Nobody was outside. Pausing for a moment, tucking behind a tree, she allowed her eyes to adjust to the darkness as she scanned the area.

A flash of white behind one home. Even at the distance and in the dark, she recognized the figure by the staff he carried in his right hand. The Shepherd disappeared into the dark thick woods, moving towards the stream that Hatch and Ben had just skirted.

"I'll lead, you follow. You do not move unless I say, and you always stay behind me. Is that clear?" Hatch directed.

Ben nodded his understanding.

The wind and rain masked the movement of her footsteps, enabling Hatch to move quickly through the woods. She found The Shepherd standing by the stream, scanning the distant horizon. Hatch was within ten feet of him.

The white of his tunic flapped in the wind, his staff planted firmly in the ground beside his right leg. Hatch made the final approach, turned to Ben, and held up a hand. He nodded and remained in place as Hatch moved forward, closing the gap between the leader of the Eternal Light and herself.

Without warning, she snatched the staff from his hand and kicked hard at the back of his legs, pulling him at the shoulder and dropping The Shepherd to the ground. She stood above him with the etched staff in her hand, and then pinned him to the ground with the staff against his chest. He looked up at Hatch in both shock and fear.

"Where is Kyla Green?"

Hatch pressed the staff hard into his sternum. The Shepherd winced.

"I don't know."

"Where were you going? Where is she right now?"

"I don't know."

"Then what were you doing out here in the storm?"

"Looking for her, calling to her, like I do every night. Moon Dancer was a child of the night. I thought that if I came here, I could call her home."

Hatch looked for deception in his words, in his body, in his eyes, and saw none. She continued to hold the staff against him but eased back on the pressure.

"I swear to you, I don't know what happened to her. I don't know where she is."

Hatch looked back at Ben. The missing girl's father's eyes brimmed with rage.

"She's here. I know she is." Hatch said.

"Where? We've looked high and low." The Shepherd said.

Suddenly, over the sound of the wind, Hatch heard a wail, but not the warning siren. This was a child's scream. Hatch pivoted and looked in the direction of the scream, uphill, and saw a blur of white heading away from the commune's main space.

The tall Mathias was moving fast. Over his shoulder, it looked like he was carrying a white sack, which, by the blonde pigtails, Hatch immediately recognized as Marigold.

"Where's he going?"

"Mathias lives just beyond the rise of that hill."

Hatch felt the weight of the staff in her hand. "Get everyone to safety."

"What are you going to do?" The Shepherd asked.

"I'm going to end this." She hefted the weight of the staff. "And I'm going to borrow this."

The Shepherd, still on his back, still shellshocked, gave a nod of his head. Hatch took off in a dead sprint through the woods. She heard Ben rasp in desperation as he tried to keep up with Hatch's relentless pace.

Wind pushed hard and uprooted a tree, slamming it down in front of Hatch. She hurdled the obstacle and continued into the darkness as a funnel formed in the clouds ahead, the end reaching down from the heavens toward the ground below.

TWENTY-FOUR

SAVAGE STOOD IN THE DOORWAY AND WATCHED HATCH PEEL OUT OF THE parking lot, with Kyla Green's father in the passenger seat. The old man who ran the hotel had called for Savage to come into his shelter beneath the manager's office. Savage refused with a shake of his head and then retreated into his room and called Thorpe.

"I've got the warrant drafted. Ended up stopping at home and doing it there rather than going all the way into the office. But it's done. Told you I was faster on the paperwork than I am on the draw. I just need to head in to get this signed. Not sure I'm going to be able to get a judge tonight, though. Heck, I'll be lucky to get ahold of a supervisor. Whole county's shuttin' down. Best get yourself below ground and weather the storm. We're gonna have to find us a judge in the morning."

"That's not why I'm calling. How fast can you get here?"

"That wind in the background is making it hard to hear, but did you make it back to Jericho Falls? You know they just upgraded the tornado warning?"

"I need you to get me. Turn around and pick me up." Savage raised his voice above the howling wind outside his door.

"Why? What's happening?"

"My friend."

"The reporter?"

"She's not a reporter," Savage said bluntly.

"Then what is she?"

"She's a storm of her own making, and she's about to unleash hell on the Eternal Light, and we need to get there, now."

" I'm not far from you. I just stopped to check in on my aunt, just south of Mt. Juliet. I can be at your motel in less than ten. I'm on my way."

Savage heard the screech of Thorpe's tires and the roar of the Chevy's engine before hanging up.

THORPE'S SUV skidded to a stop on the gravel of the lot in front of Savage's motel room. Wind and rain created a barrier to his progress. In the ten seconds it took him to get from the roof's overhang to the Chevy's passenger side, Savage got doused with enough rain to soak him through his clothes. Before the door was completely shut, Thorpe was already accelerating down the windy drive toward town.

The roar of the engine couldn't be heard above the wet wind slapping the Suburban from all angles. "This is bad," Savage called out across the center console to Thorpe who held the wheel with a death grip as he tried to control the violent jerking of the heavy SUV.

"Bad? This is just the warmup round." Thorpe looked over at Savage through fogged glasses. He turned his attention back to the road ahead.

The SUV's wipers worked overtime and did little to aid their visibility. But Thorpe raced ahead at speeds that, to Savage, would have felt fast in optimal conditions, not in the middle of what Savage could best describe in two words: toilet bowl. And it felt like they'd been flushed.

Just outside of town, a downed tree blocked the road. Savage cursed under his breath and stuffed a handful of black licorice bites into his mouth.

Thorpe sat calmly behind the wheel and wiped the fog from his glasses with the bottom of his sweater vest. He then slid them back in place and looked at Savage. "Better make sure you're buckled. It's about to get a little bumpy."

The SUV swerved to the right as Thorpe took it off-road. Tires spun over loose soil, soaked in the torrential downpour. The Chevy's tires rumbled over broken tree limbs and rock. The off-road adventure circumvented the obstacle and Thorpe brought the vehicle back onto the main road.

"I may look like Ned Flanders, but I drive like Richard Petty," Thorpe said as they set off again. Spotting the break in the road leading to the Eternal Light's commune, Thorpe took the turn hard and the back end fishtailed on the muddy path as they rounded a bend of trees.

The front gate was closed. Instead of slowing to a stop, Thorpe floored the gas pedal, bringing the roar of the eight-cylinder engine to life.

"Brace yourself."

Savage checked his seatbelt and looked wide-eyed at the unassuming Wilson County Sheriff's detective.

"I guess if we're going to break some rules, we might as well break some fences." Thorpe said just before barreling into the front gate at full speed. The wooden brace on the opposite side cracked like thunder. The boards of the gate snapped and splintered. Wood boards peppered the front end of the Suburban, spidering the glass of the windshield as they broke through to the other side. The front end took a beating, but the engine was still running. A trickle of steam led out from the fold in the hood.

Standing between the two columns of wooden homes was The Shepherd. He was frantic and flagged them, waving his arms above his head wildly as a funnel cloud formed in the distance behind him. Thorpe slammed the vehicle to a stop and Savage jumped out with his gun at the low ready.

Thorpe, with his sidearm, came up alongside Savage, his gun drawn. They kept their weapons low as they approached The Shepherd, who kept his hands high at seeing the weapons. When they got close, they could hear his voice above the wind.

"Mathias! It's Mathias!"

Savage remembered the tall, tongueless man. "Where's Hatch?"

The Shepherd pointed past the commune's main space. "Over that ridge! It's Glen Miller's old place. Mathias... I didn't... I didn't know."

Savage and Thorpe holstered their weapons and took off at a run in the direction The Shepherd had pointed.

TWENTY-FIVE

HATCH CRESTED THE RISE OF THE WOODLAND. RAIN FELL IN SHEETS, THE sound of which was drowned out by the roaring wind. Just as The Shepherd had said, a small cabin sat less than a football field's distance away. The trees surrounding the cabin had been cleared. There was no sign of Mathias. Hatch listened but heard nothing but rain and wind. No longer were the girl's screams heard above the howl.

The roof's pitch flattened at its center. The roof itself overhung a front porch supported by thick wooden beams. Smoke rose from the stone chimney in the rear of the structure. Three steps led to a wood plank wraparound porch and the front door beyond.

"Listen, it's probably best if you stay here."

Hatch had to yell for Ben to hear her above the wind. Her request was met with a defiant look. His hair blew wildly as he shook his head no.

Not wasting precious time in arguing, she instructed, "If you're coming, stay behind me and let me work."

Ben nodded. Hatch ran down the slope of the small hill, slipping on the loose ground, catching the trees with her free hand while the other balanced The Shepherd's staff. Ben lagged about fifteen feet behind.

Hatch moved up the wooden steps and onto the porch. She readied the only weapon available to her at the moment, The Shepherd's staff. Hatch brought her right hand up high on the staff and kept her left at her waist. Ben lumbered up the steps behind her, holding his side and wheezing.

"Check the door. See if it's open." Hatch brought the low end of the staff up and in line with the middle of her chest as Ben moved his hand to the door's handle. Just before he reached it, a gust forced the door inward like an invisible battering ram. It slammed against the inside wall with a loud bang.

Hatch followed the wind as if it were a point man, swooping inside and visually clearing the space in front of her. The room was of simple design. It had a small living and kitchen area that flowed together as one. Against the far wall was a stone hearth where a fire roared from the blast of wind. In front of the hearth was an oval handwoven rug.

In Hatch's rapid visual sweep, she saw a solitary room to her left, the only place in the cabin's interior separated from the room where she stood. The door was closed.

Hatch took the staff with both hands, leading with her left. Like a primitive hunter on the prowl, she approached the closed door. She heard the crackle of Ben's wheeze as he took up behind her. "Check the knob."

Ben moved around in front of Hatch. Water dripped from his rain-soaked clothes onto the dusty wood of the floor in front of the door as he reached out and tested the lock. With his hand firm on the knob, Ben turned to Hatch and with his other gave a thumbs up, indicating it was unlocked.

Hatch listened for a moment. Hearing nothing but the wind and rain, she took two quick breaths and prepared her mind for battle. Hatch gave a nod to Ben, who turned the knob. Dynamic entry was the best way to overwhelm an opponent. With the door open, Hatch kicked out hard with her right foot. The bottom of her boot slammed into the door near the knob and, with a force equal to the wind, smashed it wide.

Hatch entered the tight space, leading with her staff. Using her shoulder to pin the door to the wall behind it, an entry tactic to negate any threat that might lurk there. Keeping the door pressed to the wall, Hatch immediately saw the room contained nothing but an empty bed and a nightstand. No sign of Mathias or the girl. She turned to see the desperation in Ben's eyes as he stood at the door.

"Maybe he didn't come to the house. He must have them somewhere else." Ben's words came between raspy coughs. "Maybe he ran out the back?"

Hatch stepped in to the main space and lowered the staff, pinning it along the right side of her body. She looked at the back door of the cabin. The door was closed. With the rooms now cleared, Hatch took a second to closer inspect her surroundings. She looked back to the front door where they had come in. Wet footprints from their shoes marked the path of their entry and sweep of the cabin. Another set of prints, with no tread markings, followed their initial path, but detoured toward the fireplace, disappearing into the braided rug on the floor in front of it. No prints led to the back door.

Ben followed Hatch's eyes around the room. "They sure as hell didn't disappear up the chimney."

"Maybe there's a door hidden along the back wall in the kitchen area." Hatch spoke louder than she would've under normal conditions, but the background noise was deafening, forcing her to yell to be heard above it.

"I'll check out back." Ben moved toward the rear of the cabin.

Hatch made her way over toward the hearth. She looked down at the carpet. "Wait!"

Ben hustled back and stood beside Hatch. She pointed down to the rug. "The tracks don't cross over. They stop here, just beyond the border."

Hatch bent low, the staff now serving to balance her deep squat. Just as she and Ben grabbed the bristly edge of the rough carpet and prepared to move it, they heard a scream pierce through the flooring where they knelt. Hatch and Thorpe jerked the rug aside and saw a trap door access panel. "Ready?" Hatch gripped the rope handle connected to the closed hatch. She didn't look back at Ben as she said it. Her focus was on the door and what lay beneath its wooden planks.

"Ready as I'll ever be."

Hatch yanked the braided rope handle upward. A flicker of candle-light from somewhere below illuminated a dirt floor ten or so feet underground. A rope ladder was pegged into the floor joist. Hatch descended the ladder, following it down to the hard ground. Ben followed close behind. Hatch strained her eyes as she scanned the dimly lit cellar.

The basement where she and Ben now stood was smaller than the main floor above. It was damp and much cooler than topside. She could taste the dirt in the air and it filled Hatch with a disquieting feeling.

Wax dripped from a candle on a far wall that provided the only light in the room. A shovel and axe rested in the corner to her far left. For a split second, Hatch considered swapping the staff for the bladed edge of the axe, but decided to keep the weapon already in her hand. Years of martial arts and combative military schooling made the staff her most familiar weapon of choice.

Ahead, roughly where the hearth above was located, Hatch saw a closed door. Just as before, Ben opened the door while Hatch stood ready for the threat.

The door opened to a long, dark hallway. At the far end, thirty feet away, was a candle much like the one in the room before. The light cast revealed a bend in the path.

She crept forward in the low light, passing through the narrow hallway carved in the dirt. Thick 4x6 wooden beams, like the ones supporting the rooftop, served as braces for the tight space. Halfway down the hallway on the right was a door. Hatch had just enough light to see that it was ajar.

She approached quickly but cautiously. A plank of wood lay on the ground nearby. The door opened outward. Hatch pressed herself against the mud-packed wall and peered through the two-inch gap of the open door. Light danced on the wall, casting strange shadows. She could feel Ben's breath on the back of her neck as he took up his position behind her.

She listened intently. A strange metallic knocking came from inside the room. Hatch gave herself a two count before using the staff to swing the door the rest of the way open.

Stepping inside, button hooking to the right to clear the room in one swift move. Nothing. The room below was much like the one above, except the bed in this room was merely a haystack covered in a linen sheet. A broken bit of crusty bread and an empty glass sat on a table next to it. At the far wall on another table, the source of the metallic clacking was identified. A Newton's cradle banged away, oblivious to the calamity around it. Hatch spun on her heels to face Ben standing in the doorway. His face displayed the anger and frustration Hatch felt.

"She's alive. I know it!" Ben's voice cracked in desperation.

Hatch was already moving toward the door when a shadow appeared behind Ben. In the dim light, the tall, thin figure and dark, brooding eyes of Mathias met her gaze.

"Ben, watch out!"

Ben had only managed to pivot halfway, partially turning himself to the oncoming threat, but it was too late. The large fist of Mathias struck Ben on the side of his head, just beneath his temple.

Hatch rushed forward. The impact from the punch sent Ben tumbling into the room and colliding hard with Hatch, head-butting her in the chest and knocking her back. Hatch recovered, pivoting on her back foot and sidestepping out of the way as Ben fell forward onto the ground at her feet. He landed face first on dirt, unconscious.

Hatch scrambled for the open door as Mathias pulled the door closed, and she heard the wooden brace wedge against it.

She rammed her shoulder into the closed door, but it wouldn't budge. Hatch turned to Ben, now sitting up but still shaking off the effects.

"Get to your feet, soldier. We've got to find our way out of here. Fast."

TWENTY-SIX

Hatch ran full speed from the middle of the room, slamming her shoulder hard into the door. The wood made a loud cracking sound, but the door itself didn't budge.

"Look around the room. See if you can find something to get some leverage on this door."

Ben was now on his feet, still half-dazed from getting cold cocked. He went over to the table where the cradle banged out its rhythmic cadence. Upending the table, he knocked the cradle to the dirt floor, silencing it. He then kicked hard, snapping off one of the table legs.

"You think this will work?" Ben held it up.

"Too wide, just like the staff. I need something thinner, like a wedge."

Hatch searched around the bed. The legs of the nightstand were smaller than the kitchen table's, but still not thin enough for her to wedge into the crack between the door and its frame.

Ben moved across the room and stood facing the wall beside the door. He let out a guttural howl and slammed the broken end of the table leg into the hard-packed earth wall. Hatch watched as Ben began hacking away at the wall, using the table leg as a makeshift shovel.

"It's dirt, right?" he called over his shoulder. "Maybe we can dig our way through."

Seeing no better option, Hatch cinched her grip on The Shepherd's staff and began pounding into the dense earth with the bottom end. The dirt broke free and fell in small clumps at their feet as they hacked away.

Ben worked in a frenzy, at one point abandoning the wood leg altogether to claw at the dirt wall with his hands. Hatch smacked hard with the staff. Dirt fell between the boards above her.

"Maybe if we thin it out enough, I can ram through it with my body."

They were making headway, caving in several inches on the dirt wall. Hatch gauged it at least a foot thick. It was tedious work. Worse than that, they were losing precious seconds. At the midway mark, they encountered roots and rock that served as a natural rebar and making it nearly impossible to dig through.

Hatch raised the staff back and prepared to deliver another strike when she heard a noise coming from the other side of the door. She gripped Ben's shoulder, putting a temporary halt to his relentless digging. He hadn't heard it, lost in his frenzy. Hatch held her finger to her lips.

Positioning herself dead center in front of the door, she tucked the staff underneath her right side. With her left hand angling the long stick's end toward the threat, Hatch took a deep stance, preparing to thrust forward the moment it opened.

She heard the brace release its hold on the closed door. A second later, the door swung wide. Standing in the dimly lit hallway, were Savage and Thorpe side by side, guns drawn, and pointed at Hatch. Savage's face released some of its tension at seeing Hatch. Thorpe, the unassuming Wilson County detective, still wore the sweater vest she'd seen him in earlier, but behind the glasses Hatch saw the eyes of a lion. At seeing Hatch and Ben, they lowered their weapons.

"Where is he?" Hatch asked.

Savage raised his shoulders in a shrug. As if answering Hatch, a scream came from around the bend in the hallway, floating just above the howling winds, shaking the foundation of the house above.

"Help! Help me!" The scream came, and Hatch recognized the source. The young, happy-go-lucky, flower-loving Marigold.

Hatch and Ben joined Savage and Thorpe in the hallway, and the four moved fast, the narrowness forcing them into a staggered single file led by Savage. Hatch and Thorpe were nearly shoulder to shoulder behind him. Ben brought up the rear, still carrying the broken table leg like a pinch hitter taking the plate.

They crossed the ten feet to the turn where the candle illuminated the far end. Twenty feet away, muted by darkness, they saw Mathias preparing to ascend a wooden staircase towards a double door hatchway at the top.

"Stop! Police!" Savage shouted. "Let the girls go!"

Mathias didn't turn. Kyla Green was slumped over his right shoulder, hanging halfway down his back. She craned her neck up and screamed. Marigold was being dragged by the sash she wore around her waist.

The blonde's pigtails whipped wildly as she twisted and squirmed. She leaned her bodyweight forward and dug her feet into the dirt below, pumping her arms like a sprinter. He tugged the sash, jerking her back towards the stairs.

"I don't have a shot," Savage said.

"Me neither. The kids!" Thorpe responded, both men keeping their eyes trained down the front sight of their firearms.

Hatch stood a half foot back, wishing she had one of her own, wondering if she would've taken the shot. But Kyla's body blocked Mathias's vitals, and the bend of her back covered most of his head. His arm secured her legs at the knees, holding them tightly against his chest.

He rammed his shoulder into the hatchway door, tried to push it open while keeping his other hand on the scrambling Marigold. He leveled a hard left shoulder into the seam between the two doors and it sprung wide. Wind filled the tunnel.

Hatch felt the wind's force pushing her back. The gust dowsed the candle in the back corner. The gray swirling clouds outside provided the only source of light.

Hatch sprinted forward between the two armed lawmen and ran at Mathias. Mathias ascended the stairwell, dragging Marigold up the steps, kicking and screaming. Hatch was close, nearing the bottom. Her foot hit the first step when Marigold's sash broke. She came hurdling down. Dropping the staff, Hatch caught her and the two fell to the dirt below.

"I got you," Hatch said. "Stay here."

Hatch grabbed the staff and got to her feet. Dashing for the stairs, she saw Mathias, silhouetted by the gray swirling clouds above. The winds howled as he slammed both doors shut. Hatch launched at the opening, but just before her right shoulder slammed into the seam between the doors, Mathias slid a board between the outer handles, stopping Hatch's momentum.

She slammed into it, sending pain down her right arm. She felt the tingle across the old scars, and the rage built inside her like a tempest. The impact knocked her back a few steps.

Regaining her footing, she pressed her left shoulder hard against the left side door, creating enough of a gap between the two that she could work the staff in between. Savage and Ben rushed to her aid. Thorpe tended to Marigold. Savage climbed up the stairs and put his own weight behind Hatch's.

"If we could get just enough, we can pop this thing open."

Hatch worked the staff, pressing hard, trying to add additional leverage, working it like a fulcrum. She pulled the staff while leaning against the door, grunting hard with the exertion. She heard a crack, but it wasn't the door. It was The Shepherd's staff.

It snapped in two at the midway point. Hatch fell back into Savage, and the two tumbled down the short flight of stairs, landing in a heap on the hard packed dirt below. "The axe. I saw it in the corner of the first room we passed through."

"I'll get it." Savage retreated into the darkness.

Hatch eyed the door that had denied her. She took the jagged end of the broken staff, now whittled down eight inches, and jammed it back into the gap. Hatch then reapplied the force of her shoulder to the left door of the hatchway.

"We've got to go back out the front." Ben took over helping with Marigold as Thorpe took the lead.

"I'm going to keep working the door." Hatch rammed her left shoulder into the resistant wood blocking her exit. Just as the group was about to pass the bend where the candle had been, Savage appeared in the darkness.

Savage passed the others and ran to Hatch. The axe she'd seen before was in his hand. Holding the handle at his shoulder near the butt end of the head, he said, "Let me give it a whack."

Just as Hatch retrieved the broken shard of staff from the gap between the doors, she heard a sound like a massive combine churning the ground above. The dirt walls of the hallway shattered, sending bits and pieces of debris flying and choking the air with dust.

Before taking a step down, Hatch heard the crack of wood behind her and turned. The two doors ripped free from their hinges and disappeared into a whirl of gray and dirt as churning winds attacked the world outside. Without giving a second thought, Hatch ran for the opening, knowing the distance between there and Mathias was a shorter one than retracing their steps through the cabin and out the front door.

She ran up the stairs. Savage, showing no hesitation, pursued her. Hatch burst through into the chaos of the swirling world above ground. She turned back to see Savage at the bottom of the stairs, preparing to ascend.

The wind's force was unlike anything she had ever felt before. As soon as Hatch was above ground, she was down, pressed on all fours as winds lashed out from all directions. Hatch tucked the broken staff into her belt at the small of her back and crawled to the edge of the opening. She reached an arm in to help Savage up just as a loud crack sounded from somewhere close by in the darkness.

Hatch heard it coming, the snap and crack of branches hitting branches as a thirty-foot tree fell across the opening. She roll out of the way, through soft mud and grass slick with rain. Leaving her alone with the wind and the Twister Man.

She scanned the darkness and saw his white tunic like a beacon. He was setting a wooden ladder against the roof's edge. Kyla Green, bound at her wrists and ankles, was slumped at his feet.

The world around her churned, as Hatch set out against the wind to face off with the Twister Man.

TWENTY-SEVEN

Hatch's face was peppered with the dirt and debris filling the churning air around her. Head down, she pressed forward. Mathias was up ahead, fighting his own battle against the wind as he attempted to stabilize the ladder against the rooftop. He then bent low, scooping the slumped child up onto his right shoulder. Kyla hung over his back. Her head swinging by the braided rope belt cinched around the Twister Man's waist.

Mathias gripped the side of the ladder with his left hand, stabilizing it against the rooftop. He planted his sandal on the lowest rung and prepared to climb.

As Hatch closed the distance, a blur of white appeared from around the front of the cabin. In the tumult, Hatch first thought it was Savage or one of the others. But through the whirling wind, she recognized The Shepherd.

Hobbling toward Mathias, his hands in front of his face, bracing against the swirling gusts. The going made more difficult without the use of his staff. He staggered his way forward. Mathias stopped his efforts and turned his head toward the Eternal Light's leader. The Shepherd now stood only a few feet from Mathias.

She heard the boom of his voice as she had heard when he delivered his sermon. Though she could not discern his commands, she could see the pleading desperation in his eyes as he confronted Mathias.

Hatch was less than ten feet away when a small tree branch struck her from behind. The leafless limb struck the back of her legs, upending her and sweeping her to the muddy ground. Regaining her feet, she watched the two men face off.

Ahead, Hatch saw Mathias momentarily release the grip of his left hand holding the ladder. Mathias moved toward his front waistline with his freed hand. A split second later, he produced a knife. He held it in front, aimed at The Shepherd. The blade itself was approximately six inches, curving upward at the tip.

The Shepherd raised his hands, the same pleading look in his eyes, this time begging for his own life. Mathias punched out with the blade. The Eternal Light's leader attempted to block the attack by raising his hands, but the sharp edge found its mark. Mathias retracted the weapon and tucked it back into the front of his tunic. He tightened the belt, holding it in place before continuing his ascent of the wooden ladder. With Kyla on his back, Mathias pressed upward rung by rung.

The Shepherd staggered back as Hatch closed the gap. Both of his hands pressed firmly against the left side of his upper chest, his eyes wide with fear. His linens absorbed the red of his blood. The Shepherd dropped to his knees and fell face first into the muddy earth as Hatch reached the base of the ladder.

Mathias was already halfway up with Kyla a dangling sack of white. Ben's daughter's eyes met Hatch's as she lifted herself off the rain drenched tunic of her abductor.

Hatch launched herself upward. She grabbed hold of Mathias's right leg below the knee with both hands. His skin was wet with rain and slick with mud. Hatch's grip worked against the slippery surface of his flesh. Her hands lost their purchase and Hatch slid down to his ankle. With the leather sandal strap wrapped around his foot serving as a backstop, she leaned back and pulled hard.

Mathias looked under his arm at Hatch while he held firm to the ladder and kicked hard with the leg Hatch so desperately clung to. The worn wooden bottom of his sandal came within inches of Hatch's nose. The flailing foot may have missed its mark, but the violent movement of his right leg worked to free his sandal from his foot.

Hatch fell back onto the muddy ground next to The Shepherd. The hard wood of The Shepherd's staff still tucked in her belt, stung her lower back. Golf ball sized hail pulverized the landscape. Hatch raised an arm in defense against the attacking ice pellets. She looked around her forearm shield and through the hail to see the sandal-less Mathias climb the final rungs of the ladder to the rooftop.

Just as Hatch pushed up, a violent whirl of wind ravaged the ground, sliding her across the hail-covered ground and away from the ladder. The winds rolled her to her stomach and continued to push Hatch further from the cabin. She reached to the small of her back and retrieved the broken end of The Shepherd's staff.

Hatch raised the wooden shard and plunged its jagged end into the upturned ground in front of her. She buried the wood deep and grabbed tight with both hands as winds clawed at her, trying without success to pull her further away from her destination. From Kyla.

Hatch held her ground against the storm, her knuckles white. The ladder, without Mathias's weight on it, blew from the side of the house and passed over Hatch's prone body. It sailed through the air like a wooden kite. The handcrafted wooden ladder was obliterated when it smashed into the trunk of a nearby tree.

The winds shifted their direction, enabling Hatch an opportunity to get to her feet. She looked over to where the wind had pushed The Shepherd's body. He was folded against a stack of firewood near the front corner of the cabin. He remained motionless aside from the wind that whipped his blood-soaked tunic.

Mathias stood wide-legged, bracing himself against the wind, and looked over the edge and down at Hatch. In the distance, another funnel cloud formed. The tail reached down from the angry sky and snaked its way toward the cabin, obliterating everything in its path.

Hatch locked eyes with Mathias for a moment before he disappeared.

TWENTY-EIGHT

THE BARRAGE OF HAIL ENDED, GIVING WAY TO HEAVY RAINS. WATER
flooded off the pitch of the roof. Hatch stood on the wooden planks of
the porch and looked at the rooftop's overhanging edge where the
ladder had been only moments before.

As she looked at the challenge ahead, her mind flashed to the
forty-foot tower at the BUD/s obstacle course she had tested herself
on earlier in the week. She then remembered Banyan's advice on how
to tackle the obstacle's hurdle. The roof's edge was barely within
fingertip's reach when Hatch stood on her toes to gauge the jump. She
bent her knees low, her muscles pulsing. Hatch sprung upwards,
exploding from the wet porch wood. She reached out with both hands
while airborne. The tips of her fingers clawed at the wet wood and
found purchase on the edge's lip, a wooden gutter that extended two
inches along the length of the roof.

Using the momentum of her jump, Hatch slung her legs outward
as she flipped her upper body. Swinging both legs up and over the
edge, her waist struck the edge of the roof as her body folded and her
legs fell flat against the wood. Just as she pushed herself up, she saw
Savage and Thorpe appear on the ground below.

She met the Hawk's Landing sheriff's eyes and saw the worry behind them as she pushed herself up. Savage called out to her, but she only saw his mouth move, the words carried away by wind. Hatch turned toward the top and, staying on all fours, climbed her way up.

Hatch reached the angled slope of the top portion of the roof. Long boards stretched lengthwise from front to back. Hatch took up a wide, low crouch, balancing herself against the wind along the four-foot-wide swath of the center. She faced the rear, where the stone chimney added smoke to the whirling air.

At the base of the chimney, Hatch saw a horrifying sight. Kyla Green, still bound at the ankles and wrists, lay with her back flattened against the roof boards, twisting and writhing to no avail. Mathias straddled the child at the waist, his knees pinning her tunic to the rooftop a few feet from the chimney stack.

The same blade used to stab The Shepherd, now coated in his blood, was raised high above Mathias's head. Long arms extended upward into the swirling gray of the smoke injected wind. Both of his large hands were wrapped around the wood handle. He was momentarily still and the blade, through the circling air, hovered above Kyla's chest.

Hatch ran the length of the level platform and slammed into Mathias's back like a linebacker in an open field tackle. Her right shoulder collided with his spine. The impact from Hatch's body sent Mathias face first into the stone of the chimney. He let out a bone-chilling cry that rose above the wind and the knife fell free from his hands, sliding halfway down the right side of the roof.

Mathias slumped sideways. Hatch saw blood pour out of the shattered nose of the killer. Stunned by the blow, he tumbled forward and off to the side, following the same path as the knife and coming to a stop a foot above it. He remained face down and unmoving.

Hatch seized the moment, grabbing Kyla and pulling her away from the unconscious Mathias and over to the front where the ladder had been. She quickly undid the ropes binding the girl's wrist and ankles and crawled along next to Kyla, who scooted on her bottom to the edge. Hatch leaned over the rim where Savage and

Thorpe waited on the ground below, holding their arms up to receive her.

Taking Kyla by her trembling hands, she saw the terror in the girl's face. "It's going to be okay," Hatch said. "They're going to catch you."

Kyla nodded. Hatch guided her, turning her with her back to the wood line and leading her feet first over the lip of the roof. Hatch lay flat against the roof and, holding the girl by her wrists, lowered her down to Savage, who caught the child in his arms.

Just before she could make her own descent, Hatch felt a vice-like grip on both of her legs just above the ankles. Before she could react, she was pulled back up to the flattened portion of the roof.

In a fury of rage, Matthias grabbed Hatch and tossed her like a rag doll. Hatch landed on her back. She felt the wooden shard of The Shepherd's staff still tucked in the back of her waistband. Before she could reach it, Mathias was on top of her, pinning her as he had done Kyla.

The same strong hands that had hoisted her up and tossed her now gripped around her throat. Hatch slammed down hard with both her forearms against his, trying to break the grip. She bucked her hips and tried to sweep the man off to the side, but he held firm. The howling wind seemed to subside, as the blood and oxygen to Hatch's brain became restricted. She knew she only had seconds before she'd be out cold. Mathias then reached behind his back with his right hand. Hatch saw the glint of the blade as it swept upward.

Hatch worked her right arm behind her back. The scar that stretched the expanse of it rubbed against the rooftop as she finagled her way under her back. She gripped the end of The Shepherd's staff firmly in her hand.

Mathias roared like the tempest surrounding him. Just before he brought the blade of the knife down, in one swift move, Hatch extracted the wooden shard and plunged its jagged edge into the center of Mathias's chest cavity, just below the sternum.

The curved blade fell from Mathias's hand. His death grip released. Hatch gasped in oxygen as Mathias fell to her side. Hatch gave a half roll, separating herself, then pushed back to her feet.

Maintaining a wide stance, she now stood at the center of the roof. Mathias slumped against the chimney, his head down, but only for a moment before he pressed himself up to stand.

He looked down at the wood of the staff buried deep in his chest. Then his eyes rose to meet Hatch's. She saw nothing in them but death. His face twisted in anger as he staggered forward. The deafening roar of the massive funnel closed in on the rear of the cabin.

Mathias continued his stagger forward, oblivious to the whirlwind behind him, focused on one thing. Hatch.

She bladed her stance and bent her knees, bringing her hands to a ready position. Before Mathias could close the distance, the rooftop shuddered as the chimney disintegrated, stone and debris flying.

A large piece hit Mathias at the base of his skull. Hatch saw the look in his eyes shift from rage to nothingness. His hands went to the back of his head, and when they came down again, they were coated in the red of his blood. Mathias's knees buckled, and he fell, sliding down the pitch of the roof and vanishing over the side.

The winds ravaged the structure and the boards beneath Hatch's feet came loose. She sprinted forward and then jumped, sliding feet first down the roof's slant. She rode her wooden water slide down and over the edge.

Hatch struck the ground with bent knees, like a Parachute Landing Fall. Then she rolled to her side, the soft, muddy ground absorbing the shock of her landing.

Hatch popped tall from her roll and prepared for whatever fight was left. She lowered her hands when she saw Mathias lying face down with his arms stretched out. The force of impact from the ground had forced the jagged edge of The Shepherd's staff through his body. The serpentine infinity symbols etched along the wood poked out through his back and were now coated in the dark, thick red of Mathias's blood.

Hatch felt a hand on her shoulder and turned to see Savage. "We've got to get down," he hollered over the howl of the wind.

She rounded the front of the cabin to see that The Shepherd was still alive. His arm was draped around Thorpe, who helped carry him inside. Savage and Hatch raced to the door.

They made their way down into the cellar lair where Kyla Green had been held captive. Hatch pulled the hidden door closed, casting them in darkness as the destructive force of nature ripped through the cabin above.

TWENTY-NINE

THE HOWL OF WIND SUBSIDED. THE THUNDEROUS CALAMITY GAVE BIRTH to a numbing silence. Ben held his daughter close and offered a guiding hand as she ascended from the basement ahead of him. The tornado had torn down the cabin, leaving nothing but its foundation. Its boards lay strewn among the littered trees and debris, coating the clearing where the cabin had long stood.

Hatch reached a hand in and helped pull The Shepherd out of the hole. He'd bandaged his wound with a makeshift field dressing created from the sheet that had covered Kyla's bed of hay. Fortunately, the curved end of Mathias's blade had met The Shepherd's ribcage, forcing the blade outward rather than inward.

Hatch walked over to a pile of broken boards where Mathias had fallen. She cleared away the splintered pieces, exposing the area underneath. Her heart skipped a beat when she didn't see him on the ground where he'd fallen. Frantic, Hatch visually swept the area. Her eyes came to rest on a mass of white hovering fifteen feet off the ground and shrouded by the surrounding foliage.

Mathias's white tunic was caught up in the branches of a distant tree, the wood end of the staff still protruding from the center of his chest.

Hatch approached, with the rest following in a staggered procession behind her. They formed a semicircle at the tree's base and stared at the body suspended above. Mathias was twisted, his arms intertwined with the branches that he hung from.

Savage took a step closer, inspecting the sandal-less foot. He turned to Thorpe, who was already using his cell phone to photograph the scene.

"Looks like you've found your Twister Man," Savage said while pointing to the exposed flesh above the right ankle where several white scarred pock marks peppered the back of his calf. "Looks like Blackmore's father's birdshot had indeed found its mark."

Thorpe was speechless, but Hatch saw in his expression that a great weight had been lifted from the man's thin shoulders. The Shepherd came up alongside Hatch and leaned close.

Hatch looked at the jagged end of the broken staff protruding through Mathias's chest, then turned her attention to the holy man standing beside her. "I guess I had you pegged wrong."

"Judgement is always best left to the Lord." His voice was softer, less preachy. "I, too, may have been quick to judge." He offered a smile.

"Sorry about back there—earlier—in the woods," Hatch said.

"Under the circumstances, I'd say you put the staff to better use than I ever could." She shot a glance at what was left.

"What were you doing out there last night?" Hatch asked.

"The same thing I did every night since Moon Dancer disappeared. Walking the stream and calling out to her." The Shepherd looked over at the little girl, attached to the hip of the father she had just been reunited with.

"Shepherd." Kyla's voice was that of a songbird, lyrical and light. "I heard your call. I knew you were there in the dark."

The Shepherd bent low to receive the girl as she left her father to embrace the leader in a hug. He favored his wound as he wrapped one arm around her. Kyla peeked up from under his damp tunic and looked at him. "Shepherd, I have something to confess."

"What's that, my dear?"

"When I thought all hope was lost, I prayed to the stars. I prayed that the hunter Orion would come down and be my savior."

"There is no shame in praying to the stars. For He has made all things, near and far. To include the stars that line the heavens." The Shepherd leaned closer. "Then I have something to confess to you too."

Kyla's face drew up in surprise.

"When my prayers to bring you home seemed to have fallen on deaf ears, I cried out to the heavens and prayed to the archangel, Michael. I called upon the battle angel to descend from his perch and destroy any who may have brought harm to you." The Shepherd straightened, releasing the child back to her father as he looked to Hatch. "I called on God's most trusted soldier to bring her back. And it seems He chose you."

Marigold came and stood beside Hatch. The Shepherd patted her blonde head. "It seems that our little Marigold could see in you all along what I could not. Blind faith is a much easier leap for the mind of a child. "

The girl smiled at The Shepherd and then turned her bright eyes to Hatch. "I knew you were special that first day when I saw you."

Hatch bent low, bringing her face close to the girl's, and taking her hands in hers. "I knew you were special, too. And brave. Both of you." Hatch looked at Kyla. "So incredibly brave."

"What will you do now?" Hatch asked The Shepherd as she stood facing the tornado's aftermath on the cabin handed down from Glenn Miller to his one true follower, Mathias.

"This is one house we will not rebuild." Bending low, he reached down to the ground, picked up a long stick and set off towards the commune. "I must tend to my flock."

Hatch and the group followed him over the small hill. As they approached, Hatch saw that all ten wooden houses remained untouched. The destructive path stopped just outside the boundary of the closest shelter.

Hatch saw The Shepherd's followers slowly emerging from their homes, having weathered the storm. Dorothy Green stepped from a house and stopped dead in her tracks at the sight of her daughter walking hand in hand with Ben. She freed the Scottie nestled in the fold of her arm and the dog tore off toward Kyla. Green broke into a run as she followed close behind.

"Toto!" Kyla squealed. She bent low, catching the small black dog in her arms.

Green swooped her daughter into her arms and wept openly as she pulled her close. She looked over the little girl's shoulder at Ben and reached out an arm, pulling him into the circle.

The clouds disintegrated as light crept in from the east and the sunrise shone on a new day.

THIRTY

Hatch sat across from Savage in the same booth they'd shared the previous day, her clothes still damp from the night's storm. Hatch warmed herself with Clem's hot coffee, although another storm was brewing, and she could see it coming in Savage's eyes.

"It looks like you solved your case. Well, *cases*." Hatch said.

Savage took a sip from his mug and nodded. "Thorpe found some things in Mathias's hidden lair that proved promising. There was an old Bible, handwritten, though the additions were dark. Best we can make of it so far is Miller and Mathias sought Eternal Light by stealing the souls of those young girls at their point of transcendence."

"Sick." Hatch thought of the Rise ceremony. With the shroud of mystery lifted from the Eternal Light, she saw it for what it was, a celebration of a girl's journey into womanhood. The thought of the twisted minds capable of perverting it into something horrific would've been unfathomable had Hatch not witnessed it firsthand.

"There was a hand-drawn map in the back of the book. The dots along the map stretched from north-central Tennessee, forming a misshapen figure eight, like the infinity symbol of The Shepherd. Only one dot remained to close out the pattern."

"The cabin?" Hatch asked.

Savage nodded. "The Wilson County Sheriff's Office is going to have their hands full with dig sites. I'm going to stick around for a couple days and help Thorpe wrap some things up. You could stick around, too, if you wanted."

"I can't. I've got a funeral to go to."

Savage looked away from Hatch and down at the table between them. Picking up a butter knife, he divided the last piece of cornbread, offering half to Hatch. "You know, Clem might've been right about me."

"How's that?"

"He called me a tin man. Maybe I am."

Hatch chuckled as she took up her half of the cornbread. "Oh, really?"

Savage didn't smile. His face was serious again as he looked across at Hatch. "I've realized something in seeing you again. I need a heart. To make me whole, I need you, Hatch." Before she could form the words to respond, Savage continued. "I already know what you're going to say. But I just wanted you to know."

"Tin man." Hatch repeated the words and smiled. "If that's true, and we already have a Dorothy, then I guess that makes me the Wicked Bitch of the West."

Savage nearly spit his cornbread as he choked out a laugh. "I think it would take a lot more than a bucket of water to stop you."

An awkward silence followed the laughter as the two finished the last of the food. "Thorpe's a hell of a guy. I put the bug in his ear about coming out to Hawk's Landing when this thing is all done. Told him I've got a spot for him if he wants. There are two spots actually." He cocked his lips into a half-smile. "Any time you're ready."

Hatch felt her face warm and brought her mug up to mask it. "Things are complicated now."

"Is there someone else?"

"It's more than that."

Even indirectly answering the question, she saw the pain in Savage's face, and it crushed her.

"Aren't you ready to hang it up yet and come home? The fight is over. Every good soldier should have a homecoming. When's yours?"

"I've got to close some things from my past before I can ever truly come home."

"Then I'll wait for you. Forever if I need to."

"Forever is a long time."

"An eternity of wishing you in my life is better than one without hope."

Clem approached the table. The milk white of his mustache curved into a smile. "This is going to be it for you, Hatch?"

"Afraid so."

"Did you get your story?"

"I got to the truth."

His mustache straightened as he smiled. "I guess you can't ask for much more than that. Where's the next big story taking you?"

"That depends which way the wind blows."

Hatch said her goodbyes to Clem. He refused to accept any money from her, so she slipped it underneath her empty mug. She and Savage walked outside where Thorpe waited in his Chevy Suburban with its damaged front end.

Savage and Hatch faced each other on the curb outside of Clem's diner. His salt and pepper hair blew in the breeze and carried his familiar scent. His eyes bore deep into her soul, and she felt her heart flutter in the silent exchange between them. Without warning, Savage pulled Hatch close and kissed her.

His lips met hers. Behind the tenderness was a passion. One Hatch felt powerless to resist. The image of Cruise skirted her mind, but feeling Savage pressed against her, she relented to the power of the moment. The kiss lasted only seconds, but the sensation of it lingered.

Savage separated himself, squeezing his hands gently against her arms. "You know where to find me when you're ready."

With that, Savage turned away, looking back once before getting into Thorpe's SUV. The Suburban rattled as Thorpe drove away. Hatch's eyes followed Savage until he was out of sight.

Down the long stretch of highway, she saw a slow procession of white heading into town led by The Shepherd, walking with the help of his new staff. As they came to Main Street, white tunics broke off to the various homes and businesses lining the way and began offering help in repairing the damage caused during the night.

Hatch saw Ben Tracy among them, wearing a white tunic and sandals. He waved and smiled. Hatch greeted him. Kyla was close by with her small black Terrier on a leash beside her.

"I said I'd do anything for my daughter, and if that means joining the Eternal Light, then I will. I can't thank you enough for what you've done. Tell my brother the same and tell him I'm okay." He looked back at his daughter and Dot. "Actually, tell him I'm not the brainless wonder he remembers. For the first time in a long time, my mind is clear, and my heart is full."

"I will." Hatch eyed the tunic. "So, you're really giving this thing a go?"

" I see a future that I didn't before. As long as I'm with them, I know I can't go astray. What are you going to do now?"

"Maybe I'll try to find some of that peace for myself."

"God knows you've earned it."

Hatch said goodbye to Kyla as she and her father headed across the street. She watched the family, reunited again as the winds of change showed Hatch that anything was possible.

As she was getting into her Jeep, Marigold ran up to her. She had a fresh bouquet of flowers and handed it to Hatch.

"You are such a bright light," The girl told Hatch.

Marigold wrapped her arms around Hatch's waist and hugged her tightly. Hatch rubbed a gentle hand across the top of the girl's head, absorbing the child's embrace.

"I wish you could stay." Marigold looked up at her with wet eyes. "But I know there are others who need you. They don't know it yet, but when they cry out in the darkness, you will light the way."

The girl wiped her face. Hatch placed a gentle kiss on her head. Marigold then scurried off and took up by The Shepherd. The leader of the Eternal Light smiled at Hatch and set off for a damaged building across the way.

Hatch drove out of Jericho Falls, leaving the wake of destruction behind her.

THIRTY-ONE

THE SERMON ENDED. IT HAD BEEN ABOUT GOD'S NEED FOR GOOD soldiers and when their deeds were done, He would call them home. The delivery reminded Hatch much of what she had seen and heard from The Shepherd.

A hushed silence fell upon the small group around the casket raised above the open earth. The mourners consisted of Talon team-mates and former operators who had served with Taylor in the military Special Operations community.

Hatch's eyes rested on the widow seated in a folding chair a few feet away from her husband's casket. Her body was rigid, and she held back a tidal wave of tears, holding strong for the two young girls at each side, whose sobs penetrated Hatch's heart like an arrow.

Cruise stepped forward. His athletic build showed through his suit, his normal cocky swagger reduced by somberness. Approaching the casket, he reached into his pocket. He pulled out a shiny gold trident, the SEAL emblem pinned to operators upon completion of SEAL training, a badge of honor worn signifying their entrance into the frogman brotherhood.

It was a sacred totem honoring those underwater demolition men who gave birth to the SEAL, the gold eagle, and its trident, representing a unique symbol of eternity. Cruise raised it high in his hand, the gold plating catching the late afternoon California sun as it set. He slammed it down on the lacquered wood of the casket. A loud thud echoed, releasing the tears Taylor's widow had fought desperately to restrain. Cruise lifted his hand. The trident remained, pinned to the wood, carrying forward the brotherhood into the afterlife.

Cruise paused for a moment. A silent exchange took place between the living and the dead as Cruise rested his palm against the wood. Standing erect, he turned toward a serviceman wearing Class A and white gloves standing beside the priest. Cruise walked over and received the flag that had been draped over the casket during the service and was now folded into a tight triangle. He placed one hand on the top and one on the bottom as he took the flag.

Cruise walked to Taylor's wife and children. Each step harder than the preceding one. He stopped in front of the grieving family. He took a kneeling position in front of the widow. "On behalf of a grateful nation," Cruise's voice broke. His cobalt blue eyes grew brighter as tears formed. He extended the folded flag. The widow released her grip on her children, accepting the flag and embracing Cruise in her arms. Hatch watched as the two held each other tightly.

She thought of Graham Benson and how she had never fully repaid that debt, never looked his children in the eye, never faced his widow, never told her what really happened that day. That Hatch's hesitation had taken her husband away from her and their children.

The scar of that day that twisted its lines along her right arm from her wrist to her shoulder was nothing to the scar she carried inside, one she needed to close if she was ever to move forward.

As the service ended, Jordan Tracy approached Hatch. " I can't thank you enough for what you did for my family."

"I'm sure you'd do it for mine."

"That's how it works."

"Not that it's my place to say, but your brother is a good man. He may have had some dark times, but he's really trying to put them behind him."

"I know. My wife, Emily, and I were never able to have children of our own. She's excited about the prospect of doting on her newly discovered niece." He smiled in the direction of his wife. "We're planning a visit in the near future."

"I'm sure he'd appreciate it."

"Speaking of future…it looks like we'll be up and running soon. The incident in Alaska has been cleared by the powers that be. And that means we're back in rotation once the team has healed up. With Banyan, we'll be at full strength."

"Banyan joined up?"

"He did. He said something about wanting to work with the woman who almost bested his O-course time."

Hatch saw Banyan lingering in the crowd. Tracy moved on toward Taylor's widow. She approached Banyan, who was lingering under the shade of a tree.

"Hey, I wanted to thank you." Hatch said.

"For what?" Banyan asked.

"That tip you gave me on the O-course. It came in handy."

"How so?"

"Long story, better over a couple beers."

"The best ones always are."

"So you came on board?" Hatch asked.

"I guess I'm ready for life's next adventure. You sticking around?"

"Looks that way. For now, at least."

Hatch made her way to Cruise. The tears had been wiped from his face, but his damp lashes outlined the blue of his eyes. As he offered a half smile, she thought of Savage and the kiss he stole.

The images of the two men whirled in her mind like the winds she'd faced. The insight on which path to follow was still blurred, but she knew one thing was certain. She wouldn't be able to choose either until she had closed the rift that had left her fractured.

As the setting sun stretched her shadow across the ground, Hatch prepared for the most difficult battle yet, confronting her past.

The Rachel Hatch series continues in *Tsunami*.

Hatch seeks closure to her past
For the woman who walked through fire
Redemption comes at a price
For Hatch, that could mean her life.

Order your copy of *Tsunami* now:
https://www.amazon.com/gp/product/B09LMRFB1Z

Join the LT Ryan reader family & receive a free copy of the Rachel Hatch story, *Fractured*. Click the link below to get started:
https://ltryan.com/rachel-hatch-newsletter-signup-1

LOVE HATCH? **Noble? Maddie? Cassie?** Get your very own Rachel Hatch merchandise today! Click the link below to find coffee mugs, t-shirts, and even signed copies of your favorite L.T. Ryan thrillers! https://ltryan.ink/EvG_

THE RACHEL HATCH SERIES

Drift

Downburst

Fever Burn

Smoke Signal

Firewalk

Whitewater

Aftershock

Whirlwind

Tsunami

Fastrope

Sidewinder (Coming Soon)

RACHEL HATCH SHORT STORIES

Fractured

Proving Ground

The Gauntlet

Join the LT Ryan reader family & receive a free copy of the Rachel Hatch story, Fractured. Click the link below to get started:

https://ltryan.com/rachel-hatch-newsletter-signup-1

Love Hatch? Noble? Maddie? Cassie? Get your very own Rachel Hatch merchandise today! Click the link below to find coffee mugs, t-shirts, and even signed copies of your favorite L.T. Ryan thrillers! https://ltryan. ink/EvG_

ALSO BY L.T. RYAN

Find All of L.T. Ryan's Books on Amazon Today!

The Jack Noble Series

The Recruit (free)

The First Deception (Prequel 1)

Noble Beginnings

A Deadly Distance

Ripple Effect (Bear Logan)

Thin Line

Noble Intentions

When Dead in Greece

Noble Retribution

Noble Betrayal

Never Go Home

Beyond Betrayal (Clarissa Abbot)

Noble Judgment

Never Cry Mercy

Deadline

End Game

Noble Ultimatum

Noble Legend

Noble Revenge

Never Look Back (Coming Soon)

Bear Logan Series

Ripple Effect

Blowback

Take Down

Deep State

Bear & Mandy Logan Series

Close to Home

Under the Surface

The Last Stop

Over the Edge

Between the Lies (Coming Soon)

Rachel Hatch Series

Drift

Downburst

Fever Burn

Smoke Signal

Firewalk

Whitewater

Aftershock

Whirlwind

Tsunami

Fastrope

Sidewinder (Coming Soon)

Mitch Tanner Series

The Depth of Darkness

Into The Darkness

Deliver Us From Darkness

Cassie Quinn Series

Path of Bones

Whisper of Bones

Symphony of Bones

Etched in Shadow

Concealed in Shadow

Betrayed in Shadow

Born from Ashes

Blake Brier Series

Unmasked

Unleashed

Uncharted

Drawpoint

Contrail

Detachment

Clear

Quarry (Coming Soon)

Dalton Savage Series

Savage Grounds

Scorched Earth

Cold Sky

The Frost Killer (Coming Soon)

Maddie Castle Series

The Handler

Tracking Justice

Hunting Grounds (Coming Soon)

Affliction Z Series

Affliction Z: Patient Zero

Affliction Z: Abandoned Hope

Affliction Z: Descended in Blood

Affliction Z : Fractured Part 1

Affliction Z: Fractured Part 2 (Fall 2021)

Love Hatch? Noble? Maddie? Cassie? Get your very own L.T. Ryan merchandise today! Click the link below to find coffee mugs, t-shirts, and even signed copies of your favorite thrillers! https://ltryan.ink/EvG_

Receive a free copy of The Recruit. Visit:

https://ltryan.com/jack-noble-newsletter-signup-1

ABOUT THE AUTHOR

L.T. Ryan is a *USA Today* and international bestselling author. The new age of publishing offered L.T. the opportunity to blend his passions for creating, marketing, and technology to reach audiences with his popular Jack Noble series.

Living in central Virginia with his wife, the youngest of his three daughters, and their three dogs, L.T. enjoys staring out his window at the trees and mountains while he should be writing, as well as reading, hiking, running, and playing with gadgets. See what he's up to at http://ltryan.com.

Social Medial Links:

- Facebook (L.T. Ryan): https://www.facebook.com/LTRyanAuthor

- Facebook (Jack Noble Page): https://www.facebook.com/JackNobleBooks/

- Twitter: https://twitter.com/LTRyanWrites

- Goodreads: http://www.goodreads.com/author/show/6151659.L_T_Ryan